WINDOW
of
TIME

A STORY BY

Karen
Weinberg

WHITE MANE PUBLISHING COMPANY, INC.
SHIPPENSBURG, PENNSYLVANIA

This White Mane Publishing Company, Inc. publication
was printed by
Beidel Printing House, Inc.
63 West Burd Street
Shippensburg, PA 17257

In respect to the scholarship contained herein, the acid-free paper used in this book meets the guidelines for permanence and durability of the Committee on Production Guidelines for Book Longevity of the Council on Library Resources.

For a complete list of available publications
please write
White Mane Publishing Company, Inc.
P.O. Box 152
Shippensburg, PA 17257

Library of Congress Cataloging-in-Publication Data

Weinberg, Karen, 1950-
        Window of time : a story / by Karen Weinberg.
               p.   cm.
        Summary: While exploring the basement of his new house in
Westminster, Maryland, Ben finds an old jacket and boots that he
puts on and suddenly finds himself transported back to the time of
the Civil War.
        ISBN 0-942597-18-4 : $9.95
        1. United States--History--Civil War, 1861-1865--Juvenile fiction.
[1. Time travel--Fiction. 2. United States--History--Civil
War, 1861-1865--Fiction. 3. Maryland--Fiction.]   I. Title.
PZ7.W43614Wi   1990
[Fic]--dc20   90-20856
                                                                                      CIP
                                                                                       AC

PRINTED IN THE UNITED STATES OF AMERICA

AUTHOR'S NOTE

The Civil War is one of the most interesting periods of time to study. Most of us living today in the United States have ancestors who participated in Civil War battles. The locations where important Civil War events took place are familiar to many of us. It is not difficult to imagine ourselves in the shoes of the Civil War soldiers. In some regions of our country, people still cling to their Northern or Southern loyalties and continue to label people as Yankees or Rebels. Memories of the Civil War are not dead.

I would dare to guess that far more children were affected by the Civil War than soldiers. Families were large back in the 1800's. When a father went off to war, he often left four or more children back home with their mother. Money was usually a big problem for the abandoned family. A soldier's pay was not always regular and generally not enough to keep the family living comfortably. The children frequently had to take over farm chores that had formerly belonged to the father. On route to battles, troops of soldiers often traveled through the countryside and into villages taking whatever food they could find, leaving little food behind for the women and children. The invasion of Lee's Confederate troops into Maryland and Pennsylvania gave those Union states a taste of the stress that Southern families had been experiencing for years.

Most of the characters in this story are from my imagination, but some of the people mentioned, like the Shrivers, Mr. Baughman, J.E.B. Stuart, and George Custer, really lived and had a part in Carroll County history. The last names of many of my created characters are the names of families who lived in the Carroll County area during the Civil War.

All of the major events that I included in my story are based on fact. Westminster was a Union supply station for the Battle of Gettysburg. A skirmish between J.E.B. Stuart's men and Union troops did occur in Westminster as described. The sights that the main characters observed in Gettysburg would have been the same sights that you or I would have seen had we actually been at the battle.

Writing an historical-fiction book is fun because one gets to read history books without being tested afterwards. The author can read her research books as slowly as she wants and daydream endlessly. Some of the books I found most helpful in my research were Frederick Shriver Klein's *Just South of Gettysburg*, Christopher Weeks' *The Building of Westminster in Maryland*, William G. Williams' *Days of Darkness:The Gettysburg Civilians*, Bell Irvin Wiley's *The Life of Billy Yank* and *The Life of Johnny Reb*, and the Time-Life Books' Civil War Series volume titled *Gettysburg*, by Champ Clark.

Many people helped me as I wrote this book. First of all, my children, Ben and Joe, gave me their helpful criticism as each chapter was completed. My husband, Lloyd, encouraged me and gave me hope. My sister, Sandy Grotberg, gave me the first suggestions that I needed towards making my story more acceptable to the outside world.

Ms. Janet Colburn and Ms. Linda McDaniel of the Carroll County Public Library helped to guide me toward improving my manuscript. Ms. Joanne Manwaring, Mr. Jay Graybill, and Helen Riley, of the Historical Society of Carroll County, answered various questions I had about the tiny details of life in the 1860's. Ms. Rae Leeds, Ms. Jean Hull, Ms. Dorothy Mangle, Ms. Judy Legal, and Dr. Joanne Strohmer of the Carroll County Public Schools gave their time to read my story and to recommend ways of making the book available to children. I would also like to thank Dale and Kaki Roberts for their editing suggestions.

Of course one must have a publisher to put the book into print. I was fortunate to find the White Mane Publishing Company whose owners decided to take a chance with my work and whose editors sweated over my grammar. I am grateful for their faith.

Karen G. Weinberg

CHAPTER 1

WINDOW *of* TIME

"They had no right—no right at all," mumbled Ben Leeds in disgust. Sitting on the side of his bed, he reached down to pick up the orange Nerf basketball from the floor.

"They should have asked me first before they decided to move." He sat upright and shot the ball into his trash can. It hit the rim, bounced back, and rolled under his bed. Pretending that the floor was as hot as the surface of the sun, he challenged himself to retrieve the ball without getting burned. He lay on his stomach sideways across the bed and tried to fetch the ball, but it was still out of reach. He took his shirt off and, holding it in one hand, leaned over the bedside again. He swatted at the ball with the shirt until he managed to work it towards his free hand where he could grab it.

"I can't believe Mom and Dad would rather live here in this boring little town than in the big city. I'll bet the most excitement they have around here is when everyone gets to turn their clocks forward at daylight savings time." Sitting up again on the bed, cross-legged, he shot for another basket. This time the ball swished into the basket. A brief smile crossed Ben's face. "All right! Two points." But seconds later the thrill was gone. Ben couldn't even seem to find the energy to walk over to get the ball. So much for basketball. That took all of five minutes off a long Sunday afternoon. Only 200 more minutes left until supper time.

"If they tell me just one more time that it won't be long until I love this boring town, I'll run away and live with Uncle Neal."

Ben had moved to Westminster, Maryland, only a few weeks earlier. Since it was now summer vacation, he hadn't had the opportunity to meet other boys his own age in this new town. All he could think about was how much he missed his old friends. He picked up his pillow and threw it at the trash can in frustration, knocking it over.

Then Ben heard his father calling to him, "Son, I need some help around here. Go down to the basement and get the laundry out of the dryer."

"All right," Ben answered, trying not to sound as disgusted as he felt. Working around the house was the only thing more exasperating than being bored. Ben put his shirt back on and slowly made his way to the basement door. He hesitated momentarily before descending into the dark, damp room. One thing that bothered Ben about old houses like this one was that the basements smelled of mold and spider webs—or what he imagined the odor of spider webs would be. When he flicked on the light switch, he could see the dirt floor. It was matted down from over 100 years of use. The few overhead light bulbs radiated just enough light to create eerie shadows on the moist gray stone walls.

"Creak, creak, creak." Each old wooden step gave a cry like an old man with aching bones as Ben walked down toward the clothes dryer. He opened the dryer door, trying to avoid looking at the cobwebs and dust balls scattered around the sides of the machine. His parents had not had the time to finish cleaning the house since they had moved. They had figured they would finish straightening up the more frequently used rooms upstairs before tackling the basement.

Ben emptied the dryer of its contents and carried the full laundry basket toward the steps. A sudden movement caught his eye. A tiny brown mouse skittered from under the bottom step to a pile of old boxes in one dark corner of the basement. Ben had not noticed those boxes before. Having always been curious, Ben found himself drawn to that basement corner to investigate.

"What's taking so long with that laundry, Ben?" came the demanding voice of Mr. Leeds at the basement door. "There is a lot more work to be done up here. Get moving!"

Ben sighed, turned, briskly picked up the red plastic basket, and carried it upstairs. He entered the kitchen. "Here you go, Dad," he said. "By the way, I was just thinking that maybe you and Mom wouldn't mind if I started cleaning up the basement."

Mr. Leeds was unable to hide his shock. He stuttered a bit, "W-w-w well, uh, why that's a good idea. It would probably be more helpful than some of the other jobs I had planned for you. The broom and dustpan are on the back porch. You can take a couple of trash bags down with you too." He took the laundry basket out of Ben's hands so quickly that Ben figured his dad wanted him to get started with the work before Ben lost his enthusiasm.

Ben found the broom and dustpan and headed back down the basement steps. His father stood at the top of the steps and watched Ben get started on sweeping the loose dirt and dust balls. Ben kept his eyes on his work, looking as though he was concentrating on business instead of wishing for his father to leave.

Finally, his father left, closing the door behind him. Quickly, Ben set his broom down and headed toward the mysterious boxes again. There were about fifteen boxes in all. On the top of the pile sat old ripped cardboard boxes. At the bottom of the pile were what appeared to be large wooden crates.

The cardboard box Ben reached for was easily opened, but the dim room light made it difficult to see what was inside. He stuck his hand into it hoping to feel coins, jewels, or at least some toys. He was immediately disappointed as he pulled out an old hardback book. He held it up towards the light and found it was a history textbook.

"History," thought Ben. "How boring—just like this town." He reached in again and pulled out two more identical books. Ben's interest was rapidly disappearing. "This junk must belong to Professor Henderson." The professor had owned Ben's house for the past thirty years before he died last spring. His relatives had taken all his valuable belongings out of the house before the Leeds family moved in. This pile was probably not worth their effort to move.

Professor Henderson had taught history at Western Maryland College, which was located at the western end of town. Ben's father also taught at the college, but his father taught in the music department. Ben's mother worked as a nurse at the nearby Carroll County General Hospital. She was working there today, but planned to be home in time for supper.

Ben pulled the cardboard boxes off the pile so that he could find out if there was anything more interesting in the lower wooden ones. Suddenly, the basement door opened and his father called down, "How is it going down there? Need any help?"

Ben immediately started whistling a "whistle-while-you-work" song. He interrupted the song just long enough to shout back, "I'm doing fine by myself. I'm just cleaning out some trash from this corner. It's starting to look better already."

"O.K., son. Keep up the good work. Mom will be real surprised when she gets home. I'll go ahead and put the roast in the oven. It will probably be ready in about 2 hours."

"Great, Dad," Ben responded.

When Mr. Leeds shut the door again, Ben went back to his investigating. He pulled out a large, dark blue, wooden box and realized it wasn't a crate at all. It was a very old footlocker or storage chest. It had initials painted on the front under the lock. He couldn't make out the letters clearly, but he was pretty sure the last letter was an "A" or an "H". The lock had already been broken. What great luck! Ben felt he couldn't get in trouble now. He reasoned that anything that is not locked is rightfully open to inspection.

He pulled and tugged at the top of the chest, but the damp basement had swollen the wood so that the top was held tightly to the bottom. Ben looked for a crow bar or something else that could be used for prying. He spied a large screwdriver sitting on his father's tool box. He fetched it and tried to use it to open the wooden box. Slowly, he was able to get it looser and looser. Then, 'POP', the top let go of the bottom. Ben threw open the lid and looked inside. Clothes! Ben was disappointed. This reminded him of the times his relatives had given him clothes for his birthday when he would much

Annelle Woggon Ratcliffe 1/90

rather have had the money used to buy the clothes to buy something he really wanted.

"Yuk! These clothes stink!" Ben exclaimed out loud. He couldn't see the mold growing on the cloth, but he could sure smell it. He reached in and pulled out the top piece of clothing, planning to throw it into the trash bag along with everything else in the chest. That way he would be able to use the locker for his own things once he aired it out. However, as he started stuffing the thick woolen garment into the plastic bag, he saw a gleam of metal. Ben looked closer. He carried it over to the closest ceiling light. Now he could see that he was holding a blue uniform jacket. The shining metal was a brass military button. On the sleeve of the coat were two yellow bars.

Eagerly, he raced back to the footlocker to pull out more clothes. He found some shirts, woolen pants, and several old blankets filled with moth holes. Beneath the blankets, Ben found his treasure. There lay two old canteens, an antique revolver, and a pair of stiff, crinkled, leather boots. Ben immediately picked up the revolver. Bits of rust flaked off into his hand as he turned the weapon from side to side to study it. He wondered if it was still loaded. Whether it was or wasn't, he knew enough not to point it at himself. Ben curled his right hand around the smooth wooden handle of the gun. He aimed the gun towards one of the basement lights and cocked the firing hammer, hoping to see if light passed through the barrel. That would mean there weren't any bullets in the gun. He had seen police do that on T.V. However, as Ben pulled back the firing hammer, it snapped off, spraying rust onto his face.

A feeling of guilt flooded through Ben. He looked around to make sure no one saw him as he stuffed the revolver back into the chest. He thought he would try some of the less breakable treasure. He spied the leather boots and decided they would be safe. He kicked off his own shoes and tried on the boots. They were just a little bit too big and very uncomfortable, but he was already making plans to wear them to school some day.

He decided to try on the army jacket too. He buttoned the few remaining buttons. Then he stuck his eager hands into each of the many uniform pockets hoping to find money. The two hip pockets were empty except for blue lint. Next, he patted the chest pockets and listened for the sound of loose change. Instead, he heard a crinkling sound. Gently, he dipped his hand into the left breast pocket and found a folded piece of paper. He opened up the fragile, yellowish paper. A little bit of one corner broke off and fell onto the floor. Holding the larger piece with care, Ben tried to read what was written on it, but the lighting in the basement was too dim to read the faded writing. Even holding it under the light bulb did not help.

Ben thought, *Why aren't there any windows in this dungeon? I need some sunlight to figure out this writing.* He looked around the room. It was then he noticed a board that had been nailed up high on the basement wall above where the boxes had been piled. Ben took off the jacket, put the mysterious note in his jeans pocket, and pushed the footlocker back over towards the boarded wall. He hoped there might be a window on the other side of the board. He took his trusty screwdriver and tried to pry the board away from the wall. This was even more difficult than opening the chest, but he could see he was making some progress when a few faint rays of sunshine pushed their way through the ever widening crack. Yes, it was a window.

How strange, Ben thought. *Why would anyone want to block out sunshine from such a dreary basement? Maybe Professor Henderson had something so secret in his basement that he did not want to let people look inside.*

Ben put more effort into getting the board away from the window. As with the footlocker, he was finally successful through persistence. The board popped away from the wall and landed on the pile of cardboard boxes.

Ben had to get up on the tips of his toes while balancing on the footlocker so that he could look out the window. There, in Ben's own back yard, he saw three boys playing ball. Two of the boys seemed to be about Ben's age, but the other one was younger by a few years, he guessed. The bigger boys were playing Keep Away from the smaller boy, but the boy did not seem to mind being teased. He laughed and kept trying to win the ball back.

Ben wondered, *What in the world are those kids doing in my yard?* He had never seen them before. The clothes they wore were strange. Each boy wore a tan pair of pants rolled up to the knees. Each had suspenders holding up his pants and none wore a shirt. They were barefooted.

"Hey!" Ben shouted. But the boys didn't seem to hear him through the glass in the window.

Then Ben heard a knock at the basement door. Again his father called down, "Everything all right? I thought I heard you calling."

"No problem," Ben answered as he continued looking out the window. The youngest boy was tackling one of the big boys to keep him from catching the ball. In the process, the younger boy kicked his leg up into the air, hitting the ball with his foot. Ben watched the ball fly toward his window. He ducked just in time to miss getting hit by broken glass as the ball crashed through the window pane.

The three boys howled. Ben could hear the biggest boy say, "Now we're in big trouble. Mr. Flint told us that, if we broke one more of his windows, he would let Butch get us. Run for your life!"

"Wait," Ben called out. "You forgot your ball."

But the boys seemed too panicky to hear Ben as they leaped over the yard fence to escape. The youngest entered the house that was connected to the side of Ben's house.

Almost every bit of glass had been knocked out the window. Ben had an idea. It might be a good joke on his father to crawl out through the window, give the ball back to the kid next door, and then knock on the Leeds' front door. His father would not be able to figure out how he got there without using the basement door.

Ben picked up the ball from the floor. It was a firm, small, cloth ball that seemed to have something heavy like rocks wrapped inside. Bits of frayed fabric stuck out here and there on its surface. Ben had never seen one like it. He pulled one of the cardboard boxes onto the footlocker and climbed both to get up high enough to crawl out the window. He held the ball in his teeth so that he could use both hands to help himself climb.

As he crawled through the window, he felt like he was breaking through a huge spider web, but he didn't take time to wipe it off. Once out on the lawn, Ben took a few steps toward his neighbor's house. Suddenly, he heard a loud, ferocious barking and growling. A huge black German shepherd dog barrelled out of Ben's back door and headed right towards Ben. Ben sprinted to the white picket fence and jumped over it into his neighbor's yard.

"Holy cow, where did that dog come from?" Ben gasped. His heart raced at double time. He reached his right hand over to his left arm where he had scraped himself on the fence. He touched bare skin. Ben looked down at his arm. Where was his T-shirt? Then he noticed the red suspenders over his shoulders holding up a pair of dark brown scratchy pants which were rolled up to his knees. He had been wearing blue jeans.

Ben plopped down on the ground and looked at the barking dog and then at his strange clothes. He started yelling, "Mom...Dad ...Mom," over and over again.

A man came out onto Ben's back porch, but it was not his father. This was a fat middle-aged man wearing a black suit. The man leaned over the porch railing and shook his pointer finger at Ben.

"I've told you brats a thousand times to keep your dad-burn toys out of my yard. Now you are trying to destroy my home. I'll teach you to break my window. Your parents will certainly hear from me. From now on, I am going to keep Butch in the yard. He will attack any one of you who trespasses again."

Incredible. Ben's parents had never said anything to Ben about inviting a terrible man over for the afternoon. Had his home been invaded by aliens while he was working down in the basement?

"Psst...psst, hey, you. Come in the house before you get chewed up by old man Flint." Ben turned and saw the young boy he had seen earlier. The boy stood at his own porch door and held it open for Ben. He waved for Ben to come over.

Ben obeyed. When he reached the boy, Ben asked, "May I use your phone? I need to call my parents to find out what is happening around here."

"Phone?" the boy responded, looking very confused. He shook his head then shrugged his shoulders. Instead of answering Ben, the boy asked his own question. "Where did you come from? I've never seen you around here before."

"That's just what I was going to ask you!" Ben responded. "I have been living in that house for the past three weeks." He pointed to his house.

"Are you a relative of Mr. Flint?" the boy asked.

"How could anyone be related to him?" Ben said with fury. "I have never seen that man before."

The boy suddenly smiled. "I get it. You're kidding me. Come on. Who are you? I'll tell you my name. I am Joseph James Harner."

"My name is Benjamin David Leeds, but my friends call me Ben. I promise you, I live in that house." Ben's and Joseph's homes were actually two parts of one bigger building. A wall divided the inside into two equal parts giving each family privacy from the other. Ben continued, "I don't know who that mean old geezer is and I don't know where that dog came from. May I please come in and use your telephone?"

Joseph laughed. "Telephone? What is a telephone supposed to be?"

Ben felt confused. But he was even more confused when Joseph took Ben into the Harner's house. Ben stood in an antique-styled kitchen. There was a large wood-stove that stood against one wall. A stovepipe rose out of the back of it and exited through the wall. A large pot of soup stood simmering on the rear surface of the stovetop. Heat filled the room. It must have been 120 degrees or more in the room. The floors were made of unvarnished wood with many worn spots, but it was well swept. There were cast iron pots and pans hanging from pegs on the wall. The only light in the room was the sunlight coming in through the windows. There was no ceiling lamp. The window panes seemed to have a slightly rippled surface which distorted the view of the back yard. Ben searched the walls for a phone. There was none.

"Is the phone in another room?" Ben asked.

"No, we don't have one as far as I know," Joseph said.

"Excuse me," said Ben as he pushed past Joseph, making his way toward the front door of the house. He knew right where it would be since the boys' homes were just mirror images of each other.

"What are you doing?" Joseph asked as he followed Ben.

"I'm going to the front door of my house to see if my father is there."

"I wouldn't do that if I were you. Old Man Flint will skin you alive."

Ben didn't care. He almost flew out the door and ran over to his own front door, but his attention was captured by the action on Main Street which ran in front of the house. His mouth fell open as he stood gazing at the scene.

Annelle Woggon Ratcliffe 1/90

CHAPTER 2

SUNDAY, JUNE 28*th*

Main Street had changed. Instead of automobiles inching their way from stop light to stop light, the street was bustling with dozens of large wagons being pulled by horses or mules. A few pony carts rolled by, some with children driving them. Men on horseback weaved in and out among the wagons. Ben could hear the clunking sound of wooden wheels bumping along the stony road. Horses whinnied and mules brayed as drivers shouted orders to their animals. Even the ground beneath Ben's feet had changed. The cement sidewalk had become an uneven, red brick sidewalk.

Ben thought the world around him was like an old western movie he had seen on T.V. *Where's the remote control? I've got to change the channel,* he thought. But, there was no remote control.

Ben felt tears coming to his eyes. Refusing to cry in front of Joseph, he turned to his door and knocked briskly. From the outside, his house did not look any different. This reassured him a bit. He knocked again, then called out, "Open up and let me in!"

The door flew open. There stood Mr. Flint with a sneer on his face. "Get out of here, you rascal! Get out! If I ever see your face again, I'll make you sorry you were ever born!"

Quickly, Ben yelled into his house, "Dad, help me! It's me, Ben!" In a glance, Ben could see that the painted walls of his living room had been covered by ugly flowered wallpaper. The furniture was different too. There were no signs that his family had ever been living in the house at all.

Joseph grabbed hold of the back of Ben's pants and tugged with all his might to save Ben from the forcefully sweeping arm that Mr. Flint was aiming towards Ben. "Let's get out of here!" he shouted.

Ben let himself be led by Joseph. He felt numb. He no longer understood anything that was happening. "Don't worry," said Joseph. "We'll work things out. Let's go back to my house."

Upon entering the Harners' house again, they heard a woman's voice from upstairs. "Joseph, is that you?"

"Yes, Mother."

"Please split some more wood for me. I'm going to need it to finish cooking supper," she said.

"All right, Mother." Joseph turned to Ben and said, "Come on and keep me company while I work. When we're done, we can go up to my room and play."

The boys went into the back yard. Ben saw a stack of firewood piled up in one corner of the fenced-in yard and a similar stack in his own yard. He could not remember either stack having been there the previous day. Joseph picked up an ax, put one of the pieces of wood on an old tree stump, and then proceeded to chop it into smaller pieces that could fit into the cook stove. Joseph talked as he worked.

"That old Mr. Flint gets meaner every day. He's been our neighbor ever since I can remember. When I was real little, he used to be pretty nice."

Ben could hear Joseph talking, but he wasn't listening closely. He was thinking, *That Mr. Flint is keeping me from getting to my family. What kind of sorcerer is he? I wonder if I can break through his evil power long enough to get home.*

Joseph just continued talking. It seemed to Ben that Joseph was just filling in the quiet with busy chatter. The young boy went on, "Mr. Flint's bad temper all started when the plans were being made to build the railroad from Baltimore out to Westminster. Mr. Flint owns a lumber mill on the southeast side of town. He was hoping that the tracks for the railroad would pass near his mill. His business would really have grown. It would probably have made him a very rich man."

Ben sat down on the grass and leaned his head onto his hands. He was feeling weak from worry. *Maybe I died. Maybe our house exploded and I was killed and this is heaven...or maybe it is that other place.* But there were no fires burning or people screaming. Mr. Flint was the closest thing to being the Devil. *Oh, please don't let me be dead,* Ben prayed silently. His brain was racing. He finally told himself, *Stop! Don't think anymore. Maybe if I just stop thinking I can stop being scared.*

Joseph's happy energetic talking seemed to enter Ben's brain now, and Ben felt his fearful thoughts being pulled away little by little. Joseph said, "The decision of where the tracks would run was to be made at a town meeting. Before the meeting, Mr. Flint went around from house to house and offered to pay people if they would vote to have the railroad follow his plans. Some of the people agreed to help him, but most, like my mother, refused. Mother told him that it is wrong to buy votes. At the town meeting, Mr. Flint's plan was voted down because more businesses could be served by the railroad if the tracks were run through the middle of town. Since that time, Mr. Flint has hated everyone in Westminster. I wish he would move away, but I guess he can't afford to."

Joseph continued chopping as Ben looked up to watch the boy. Pearly sweat droplets spotted the young boy's forehead, drawing Ben's attention to the brown freckles that were sprinkled about Joseph's cheeks and nose. The young boy's slender legs and arms rhythmically worked together to split the wood with surprising strength. The black curls of his hair vibrated with each blow of the ax.

Then Ben got an idea. *Maybe this kid is my key back to my family. I better stay close to him. He seems to know what to do to get along around here.*

When the job was done, the boys carried the wood into the kitchen and set it in a woodbox next to the stove. Then they went upstairs.

Joseph's bedroom was the same size and shape as Ben's room, but it was furnished more simply. There were two wooden beds set side by side. Each had a lumpy looking thin mattress covered by a sheet. There was no closet. Instead, there were hooks on the wall from which hung some of Joseph's clothes. The rest of his clothes must have been in the small set of drawers near the beds. A table stood against one wall and on it were placed a white porcelain bowl and matching water pitcher.

Joseph walked over to his window sill and picked up a carved wooden horse and two wooden soldiers. "See what my brother, Andrew, gave me for Christmas last year? Would you like to play with them?"

"Sure," Ben responded. He played with Joseph, but his mind was full of questions. "These are real nice toys. Where is your brother now?"

"He's in the Army. He volunteered when the war first broke out. He was working with my uncle, who is a surveyor in Michigan, when he decided to join the 6th Michigan Cavalry. The last time I saw him was last Christmas when the Army gave him a week off to come home. I was so glad to see him! Gosh, those Rebels don't have a chance against my brother!"

When Ben heard the word 'rebels', he assumed that Joseph was talking about the rebels in Central America. "Is your brother in Nicaragua or somewhere like that?" Ben asked.

"No, he's in Virginia, I think."

"Is your father in the Army too?" Ben asked.

Joseph looked down to the floor and was quiet for a moment. Then he said, "My father died three years ago."

Ben was not sure how to respond. He tried, "I'm sorry."

"My father was a doctor—a real good doctor. One day, he got a message that a whole family out in the countryside had come down with a disease called cholera. They couldn't take care of themselves, and all their neighbors were afraid of catching the disease, so my father went to help. Mother wanted to go, but Father wouldn't let her. Two days later, my mother went anyway because she hadn't heard from Father. When she got there, Father was burying the last member of the family. He was feverish himself, but he kept on working. Later that evening my father died."

"Did your mother get sick too?" Ben asked.

"No. I'm not sure why, but I'm mighty glad she didn't."

Ben sighed. "I don't think I could stand it if my father died."

"It's hard, but my grandfather is like a father to me now. He's a bank president in downtown Baltimore. He tried to get my mother to move into Baltimore, but she refused to leave this house because it was full of good memories of my father. Grandfather sends her money every month and then comes out to visit us several times a year. As a matter of fact, he rode the first train from Baltimore to Westminster back in '61 when he came to my birthday party two years ago."

"How could that be? You are too young to have been alive in 1961," Ben said.

Joseph laughed. "There you go again. You know I meant 1861."

Ben was silent. He thought, *If what Joseph says is true, that would make this year 1863. That would certainly explain all the strange changes in Westminster. But what would explain how I got back through time?* He pondered that question. *Maybe it had something to do with the window I crawled through. Everything changed from that point on. Maybe it's like a time machine.*

Joseph was uncomfortable with the long silence. "What's wrong?" he asked.

Taking a deep breath first, Ben asked, "Can I trust you?" Joseph nodded his head. "Then don't tell anyone what I am about to say. They would never understand."

"Cross my heart and hope to die," Joseph promised.

"This morning, when I woke up, I was living in the twentieth century. As soon as I came out of my basement window, I was transported back to the nineteenth century." He looked to see Joseph's reaction. Joseph twisted his face into a questioning look.

"That's the only explanation I can think of, unless I am just dreaming all this. Pinch me!" Ben ordered as he held his arm out to Joseph. Joseph pinched Ben. "Ouch!" Ben squealed.

"No dream, right?" asked Joseph.

"Right," Ben answered. "Looks like I have a major problem."

"I'll do all I can to help you," Joseph offered. He got right down to business. "I think the solution is to get you back through that window. But you won't be able to until Mr. Flint takes Butch away from there and that may not be for a long time."

"So what am I going to do until then? Sit in your back yard until good old Butch dies of old age twenty years from now?"

"Of course not," said Joseph. "You can stay with me for awhile. I'm sure I can talk my mother into letting you. It will be fun."

Just then, Mrs. Harner came into Joseph's room. "Did you get the firewood, son?"

"Yes, mam." His mother raised her eyebrows when she saw Ben, so Joseph quickly introduced Ben. "Mother, I would like to introduce you to a new friend of mine. His name is Ben Leeds."

"Pleased to meet you, Ben," she said as they shook hands. "Are you new to Westminster?"

"Yes, mam," Ben answered honestly.

Joseph added, "I met Ben over on the other side of town. He was helping his father try to repair the broken beds."

"Goodness, what happened to your beds?" Mrs. Harner asked Ben. Ben didn't answer. He looked to Joseph for help.

Joseph didn't hesitate. He said, "They broke during the accident."

"What accident?" she gasped.

"Well," Joseph continued, "when the Leeds' wagon was coming into town, their mule stopped right on the railroad tracks. Ben and his father tried to move the stupid mule, but he wouldn't budge. Then a train started coming. It got closer and closer. It was just about to crash into the mule."

Ben's eyes were wide in astonishment.

"Then Ben had an idea," Joseph said. "He ran behind the mule, risking a deadly kick, and he bit that mule right on her rear end."

Ben closed his eyes in disgust. Couldn't Joseph make up a better lie than that?

"You wouldn't believe the screech that animal made. He reared up and knocked Ben to the side of the tracks. Then the mule dragged the wagon lickety-split across the tracks. But the train was too close. The huge engine roared into the back of the wagon, knocking it over and breaking almost everything in it."

"What a terrible fright!" Mrs. Harner exclaimed. "You could have been killed," she said to Ben.

"Yes, mam," was all Ben could think of saying.

"Doesn't your father need you to help him now?" she asked Ben.

Ben hesitated before responding. He really hated to lie. "My parents aren't here right now."

Joseph quickly added, "That's right. They left Ben alone to watch over their new house while they ride the mule over to Hanover to buy some of the supplies that they couldn't find here in town. They said they might be gone for a day or two."

Mrs. Harner said to Ben, "I hate to see you living by yourself. Do you think your parents would let you stay here? You could check up on your house once or twice a day."

"Good idea, Mother!" Joseph beamed.

"I think my parents would be pleased to know someone like you was helping me, but they wouldn't want me to be a bother to you," Ben responded.

"Nonsense! It would be no problem at all. We have this great big house with just the two of us rattling around inside. Now, you two run along and check on Ben's house. Where did you say it was?"

"Down Main Street, that way," said Ben as he pointed in the direction of his house which was actually only on the other side of the wall from where they stood.

She added, "While you're there, leave a message pinned to the door to let your parents know where you are in case they get home sooner than you expected and start worrying about your whereabouts."

Joseph picked up a pencil and paper from his dresser, waved them in the air, and said, "Let's go."

"Wait a minute," said Mrs. Harner. "Come with me first." The boys followed her downstairs into the kitchen pantry. She handed Ben a jar of pickles and a jar of strawberry jam. "Set these inside your house as a little housewarming present from me to your family."

"You don't have to do that," said Ben.

"I want to. Go on now," she urged.

"Thank you, mam," Ben said, starting to catch on to the polite way of talking.

The boys went outside and started walking in the direction Ben had pointed. Neither said a word, fearing that Mrs. Harner might watch them and suspect they were up to something. When they got about two blocks away, Joseph led Ben down a side street. They both sat down on the edge of a horse trough. Ben almost expected a cowboy to mosey his horse on up to the trough. On this street, there was less activity than on Main. Rain started sprinkling down, but no one paid much attention. Each droplet that fell into the trough water made a 'kerplunking' sound.

"Thanks for trying to help me out with your mother, but how could you tell her such whoppers?" Ben asked Joseph as he dangled his hands in the cool water of the trough.

"I don't know," said Joseph. "Sometimes I just start talking and I never know what's going to come out of my mouth. Mother probably doesn't believe me all the time, but she goes along with it because she knows I would never lie about anything that's really important."

"How old are you?" Ben asked.

"I'm nine and a half, but don't let my age fool you. I have been the man of our house for over a year. I think that has aged me more. How old are you?"

"I'm almost twelve years old. My birthday is in two months, give or take a hundred or so years."

The boys watched the ripples in the water as the rain fell. Soon, the rain stopped. The air temperature must have been in the high eighties. It would have to rain a lot longer than this for the weather to cool off.

Ben was feeling hungry. He hummed the jingle of his favorite fast food restaurant. He would have eaten by now if he had been home. He looked at the jars of food that Joseph had set down next to the trough. "What do you suppose we should do with the food?" he asked.

"Let's eat it. You'll love my mother's jam. Wait a minute. I've got an idea. Let's take it down to the jail. I have someone I want you to meet."

"All right," Ben agreed. They started off toward the jail. Ben was fascinated by how many fewer homes there were in Westminster during the 1800's. But he was even more amazed at which buildings looked the same now as they had during his own century. He pointed one of them out to Joseph.

"I know that building. It's the courthouse, isn't it?"

"Good guess," Joseph said.

"I'm not guessing. Look. Over there is the Episcopal Church. My mom and I have gone down to the graveyard next to the church to do gravestone rubbings."

"What are gravestone rubbings?" Joseph asked.

"We put a large sheet of drawing paper over the designs on the headstones and then rub charcoal over the paper. The pattern from the headstone shows up on the paper. Mom and I have framed a couple of our favorite rubbings, and she hung them up in the

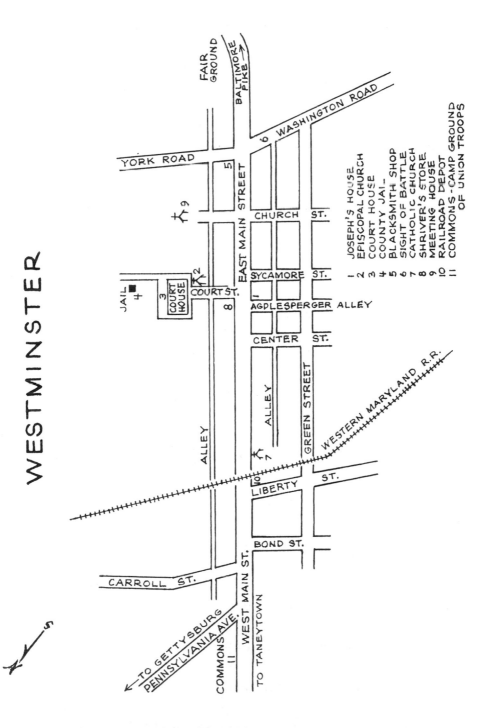

WESTMINSTER

1 JOSEPH'S HOUSE
2 EPISCOPAL CHURCH
3 COURT HOUSE
4 COUNTY JAIL
5 BLACKSMITH SHOP
6 SIGHT OF BATTLE
7 CATHOLIC CHURCH
8 SHRIVER'S STORE
9 MEETING HOUSE
10 RAILROAD DEPOT
11 COMMONS-CAMP GROUND
   OF UNION TROOPS

kitchen.'' Ben thought about his mother and wondered if he would ever see her again. He tried to force that thought out of his mind.

"Just to show you that I've been living in Westminster, I'll show you where the old jailhouse is,'' Ben boasted.

"I believe you. I believe you,'' Joseph panted as he tried to keep up with Ben, who was running in the correct direction. Joseph arrived at the jail just moments after Ben.

"See! I told you so!'' Ben rejoiced as he pointed to the two-story stone building.

"Let's go around to the back,'' said Joseph. "My friend is back there. Be real quiet, though, or we might get in trouble. We aren't supposed to be here.''

The boys tiptoed around the side of the jailhouse and kept watch for any policemen. Joseph led Ben to a barred basement window. Joseph called in a loud whisper, "Zeke! Hey, Zeke! It's me, Joseph.''

An old fellow with a long gray beard, walked from the darker part of the cell into the sunlight that entered through the window. He was scrawny, but looked happy and lively.

"Why, Joey! Come to see your old pal, did ya?'' the man said.

"I sure did. And I brought a friend and some food with me.'' Joseph introduced Zeke to Ben.

"Pleased to meet you,'' Zeke said to Ben.

"Same here,'' Ben said shyly.

Joseph opened the jar of pickles. He offered one to Ben and one to Zeke. He took one for himself. The three crunched away for a while. Then Joseph said, "Zeke, this is getting to be a regular thing now, meeting you here at the jail every few months. When are you going to stop stealing Mr. Zepp's chickens? I've told you a hundred times that I would be happy to buy you one if you really needed it."

"Now don't go lecturing me again, young man. You know Mr. Zepp and I are old buddies from back a long time ago. I just take his chickens to keep him on his toes."

"Looks like you're the one getting your toes stepped on," Joseph stated.

"Aw, I can take care of myself. Now, stop talking about me and fill me in on what has been happening out there in the world since I've been in here. The guards won't tell me anything."

"There's a lot of news about the war. I've heard talk that General Lee and his Rebels are heading this way. I think they're going to try to attack Washington. Some Union troops are in Westminster now. They have set up camp on the Commons hill at the west end of town. I think there may be some action around here soon," Joseph explained.

Ben interrupted. "Are you talking about the Civil War?"

"The Civil War?" Joseph repeated, looking confused.

"You know, the war between the North and the South over slavery."

"Yes, that's the one," Joseph said. "This war has been going on for two years."

"Heck! All this fighting is crazy," Zeke grumbled. "I wish everyone would just go back to their homes or, at least, leave Carroll County out of the war. This war has already done enough harm to the families here. Half of the people in this county are supporting the North and the rest are supporting the South..."

"Why is that?" Ben asked.

Zeke explained, "Because Maryland is right on the border between the southern states and the northern states. As a matter of fact, Maryland is below the Mason-Dixon Line, which makes it a southern state. But, since it is located north of the Union's capital, the Union Army has forced the Maryland government leaders to support the Northern cause in the war. It wouldn't do to have their capital stuck behind enemy lines."

Joseph said, "Every once in a while, we see some Confederate troops here. A few months ago, a company of Rebs came riding into town. Some folks threw a big party for them. My teacher, who is from Connecticut, went to the party hoping to see if Rebs really have horns and long tails like her family had told her. After the party, she went all over town boasting to people that she knew all along that Rebels are just like our boys. I think she even liked one of the men. She was given a couple of his uniform buttons to show to our class."

Suddenly, a loud voice came from near the jailhouse. "Hey, you little hooligans. Get out of here." Joseph and Ben jumped up as a police officer came charging after them. Fortunately, the boys had a head start on the officer.

The jelly and pickles were left behind as Joseph cried, "Follow me!" He led Ben through a small gap in a hedge of bushes behind the jail. They easily escaped because the officer was too big to fit through the opening.

When they got farther away from the jail, Joseph said, "Don't worry. That's my friend, Officer Lynch. We go through this act whenever I come around here. He and my father grew up together. He just pretends to be mad at me so that the other officers won't suspect that he is giving me special favors." By following Joseph's short cuts, the boys got back to the house in five minutes.

"I'm home, Mother," Joseph called as he swung the front door open and then closed it.

Mrs. Harner poked her head out from the kitchen. "Good. Now go out to the pump and wash up for supper. Then come in and set the table for me. We are having fried chicken, corn bread, and spinach."

Even though Ben wasn't very fond of spinach, he was so hungry that he could hardly wait to get food into his mouth, especially the fried chicken. He followed Joseph into the back yard where the pump was. Ben looked over at his own yard. There sat Butch, munching on his dinner in a bowl that had been placed right in front of the broken window. The dog looked up at him and growled. Ben quickly looked away. He thought about how worried his parents must be. Maybe they thought he had run away.

Joseph pointed to a little house in the back corner of the yard. Ben thought it might be a storage shed, but Joseph said, "There's the outhouse if you need it."

Ben blushed. "Thanks, I'll remember that."

Watching Ben try to work the pump made Joseph laugh. Ben would get excited each time the water gushed out. Ben had never enjoyed washing up so much. Back in the house, the boys and Mrs. Harner sat around the large dining room table. Joseph's mother said a blessing over the food and then the eating began.

"M-m-m-m! Mrs. Harner, you sure are a great cook!" Ben exclaimed.

"Thank you," she replied. "I think any food tastes great to growing boys like yourself." She smiled.

"Mother, could Ben and I sleep outside tonight like soldiers on a campground?" Joseph asked.

"I guess that would be all right, dear. Just make sure you don't bother the neighbors."

After the supper dishes were washed, the boys returned to the back yard. They tied a rope between two trees and hung a blanket over it. Then they tied the corners to wooden stakes that they had pounded into the ground. Joseph found a rubber tarp to lay on the ground and a couple of blankets that they could wrap themselves in if the night air should get chilly. Looking at the camp-site, Ben said, "Now all we need is a campfire and some hot dogs to roast."

"Oh, no!" Joseph gasped. "You mean to tell me that you eat dogs?"

"No," laughed Ben. "Hot dogs are a special meat that looks like sausage links, but the skin is filled with beef, chicken, or turkey. You would love them."

"You had me worried there for a minute. I have an idea. We could make popcorn over a campfire if you want to."

"Sure," Ben responded. He gathered some sticks for the fire while Joseph ran into the house to get matches, corn, and the popper. When Joseph returned, Ben saw that the popper looked like a square cake pan with a very long handled lid on it. "My family loves to eat popcorn while we are watching TV," Ben said.

"What is TV?" Joseph asked as he lit the fire with the long match he had pulled out of a metal box.

"TV means television. It is a box that has a glass screen over the front. On that screen, you can see people who entertain you."

"Are the people stuck in the box?" asked Joseph.

"No. It's difficult to explain. Watching TV is like watching movies, but on a smaller screen."

"That doesn't help me very much. I don't know what movies are."

Ben tried to explain. "Movies are stories, like in a book, but actors act out the parts in front of a camera. Then the camera records it all on film. The story can be shown to people whenever they put the film through a special machine that shines the pictures up on a big screen."

Joseph smiled. "I've seen a camera before. I had my picture taken in Baltimore last year when I visited my grandfather."

Ben gave a sigh of relief. "I never realized how many things we have in modern times that you've never heard of. For instance, look up at the sky. See all the twinkling stars? We can hardly see the stars at night where I live because the town has so many electric street lights, that their light blocks out the starlight," Ben boasted.

"That's too bad," Joseph said.

Ben had never thought of it that way. As he ate his popcorn, he looked up at the stars and saw them more clearly than he had ever seen them before.

CHAPTER 3

MONDAY, JUNE 29*th*, 1863

Ben slowly stretched before opening his eyes the following morning. He wondered if, when he opened his eyes, he would be back in his own house. But he knew he wouldn't be. He could feel the hard lumpy ground under his sleepy body and the morning breeze blowing through the make-shift tent. He opened his eyes and sighed.

Seeing that Joseph was still asleep, Ben slipped out of the tent and went to the outhouse. When he returned, Joseph was sitting up on his blanket. "Good morning, sleepy head," he said to Joseph.

"Good morning. It's my turn to use the outhouse." Joseph hurried off. When he got back he said, "Help me bring in some wood for the stove. Mother is probably up already. Wait until you taste her griddle cakes. You'll never want to leave here!"

As the boys gathered the wood, they heard heavy wagons rumbling over the stony street in front of the house. Joseph looked quizzically in the direction of the sound. "That's strange," he said.

"Why?" asked Ben.

"Those wagons were moving extra fast. Usually everyone drives slowly along Main Street. Maybe someone is having a race." But the street sounds quickly returned to normal. "Oh well, let's eat our breakfast."

As they walked into the kitchen, Mrs. Harner was entering from the other side. "Good morning, children. Did you have a good night?"

"We sure did," said Ben as Joseph nodded in agreement.

Then Mrs. Harner smiled at Joseph as she said, "Joseph, I do believe you are growing up. I didn't even have to ask you to bring the wood in."

"Aw, Maw—I mean Mother." Joseph looked embarrassed.

She laughed. "Go get cleaned up and dressed. Remember, you have some work to do at Mr. Baughman's stable. You can take Ben with you. I am sure Mr. Baughman would like to have two strong boys working for him."

The boys cleaned up. Joseph loaned Ben one of his brother's clean shirts to wear. While they were up in Joseph's room, the boys heard more speeding wagons. People were shouting in the street.

Joseph ran into the hallway and into his mother's room to look out her window which faced Main Street. He saw just the tail end of two buckboard wagons loaded with furniture and children. One of the drivers was still shouting as they disappeared into the distance. Ben had missed it all by the time he joined Joseph, but he saw people along the sidewalks talking energetically.

"Let's go find out what's happening!" Joseph exclaimed.

However, the boys were intercepted by Mrs. Harner as they raced down the steps. "Hold on there, boys. You could have an accident from running down the stairs like that. Walk, don't run, to the dining table and start eating your breakfast."

"But, Mother, something is happening outside and we want to see what it is."

"There is plenty of time for that. Now, eat!" she ordered.

"Yes, mother." Joseph said as he hung his head low.

Ben figured that his mother would probably have responded in the same way as Mrs. Harner. He wondered if all mothers through history have tried to stop their children from having fun. He obediently sat down at the table. In front of him was a six-inch high stack of pancakes. He was instantly glad that he hadn't said anything rude to Mrs. Harner. He drenched his pancakes in honey as he had seen Joseph do to his own. A large pitcher of sweet fresh milk was passed to him by Joseph's mother. "This sure is good!" he said to her after he had taken a few bites.

"Thank you," she replied. The three ate in silence.

Shortly, their attention was caught again by the sound of more rushing wagons. The shouting of men's excited voices made even Mrs. Harner jump up from the table. "What in the world?" she exclaimed as she rushed to the open parlor window. The boys took that opportunity to run out the front door. One of the wagons had stopped momentarily in front of the Harner house.

"The Rebels are coming! Run for your lives!" a man shouted from the wagon.

"Lady, save your children!" the woman in the wagon pleaded to Mrs. Harner through the open window. Then the wagon rolled on with its passengers continuing to spread the words of warning.

Joseph hollered after them, "Where are the Rebels? How many? When are they coming?" But he received no response.

Mrs. Harner saw the man who ran the shop across the street. "Excuse me, Mr. Shriver. Do you know what those people are talking about?"

"Good morning to you, Mrs. Harner. I wouldn't worry myself about them if I were you. I seriously doubt that any Rebels could be in this area. I have been told that, at this moment, General Meade and most of his troops are camped out in Frederick between Lee's troops and us. Some people will believe any rumor they hear and panic."

"Thank you. Have a good day." Then she saw Joseph and Ben. "Get back in the house, boys. The show is over. Until we know anything for sure, we will keep on with our normal activities."

They finished eating breakfast, washed the dishes, and then it was time for Ben and Joseph to leave for work. Joseph explained to Ben, "We keep our horse, Emily, in the stable behind Mr. Baughman's blacksmith shop. Instead of having to pay him, I sweep out the stable and do odd jobs for him one day a week. Mondays are my regular days."

The blacksmith's shop was just a few blocks to the east of Joseph's house. It looked about the size of a one car wooden garage, but the ceiling was higher. A man with huge shoulders stood in front of a brick fireplace holding a horseshoe with long, metal pliers. He pumped an accordion-like contraption with his foot which blew air on the fire making it burn hotter and brighter. A long, black apron protected his clothes from the flying sparks.

"Hello, Mr. Baughman. Sorry if I'm a little late, but there has been a lot of panic in town about the Rebels coming," Joseph explained.

The big man turned and said calmly to Joseph, "I think the horses have waited for you. Go back to the stable and check." He looked at Ben. "Who do we have here?"

"This is my friend, Ben Leeds. He is here to help me today. Is that all right with you?" Joseph asked. "You won't have to pay him."

"I would be foolish not to want more help. Are you ready for some hard work, young man?" he asked Ben.

"Yes, sir."

Joseph said, "Come on, Ben." He led him to the stables and introduced him to each horse, giving each a hug around the neck. He ended with his own Emily. She was a beautiful, shiny brown quarter horse. Ben had taken horseback riding lessons for a year and had learned how to tell one kind of horse from another.

"She's a beauty," Ben told Joseph. That made Joseph beam with pride.

They went right to work. Joseph handed Ben a large broom and told him to start at one end of the stable and sweep everything on the floor to the other end where the stable door stood open. Joseph grabbed a pitchfork and started picking up old straw from the horse stalls. Then he and Ben climbed up to the hayloft to get fresh straw for the horses' bedding. While they were in the loft, they heard a lot of shouting on Main Street again. By looking out the loft window, they could see over the blacksmith's shop to the street. There were about a dozen blue-coated soldiers shouting, "Clear the streets!" as they rode east through town.

"Hurrah!" exclaimed Joseph. "This is it! The Rebels are coming!"

Ben scanned the horizon for Rebel soldiers but saw none. Neither did Joseph. Instead, just a few minutes later, they saw the same Union soldiers riding slowly westward back towards their headquarters. Apparently, it had been a false alarm. The boys laughed because the soldiers looked embarrassed.

A horse whinnied from inside the stable. That reminded the boys to get back to work. They finished with the fresh bedding. From the other end of the hayloft, they scooped grain from a bin to feed the horses. Ben enjoyed holding some of the grain in his hand and letting the horses lap up the food. It felt tickley and wet. He wiped his hand on his pants when he was done.

"It looks like you are doing a good job here, boys!" came Mrs. Harner's voice. She was standing in the doorway with a straw basket hanging over one arm.

"Hello, Mother. Is it lunch time already?"

"Yes, it is. Now, wash your hands and come eat the fresh bread I made for you. I also put a jar of jam and some leftover chicken into the basket. Be sure to bring the basket home when you are done with work today. Have a good afternoon.'' She turned to leave.

"Thank you, Mrs. Harner," Ben said.

"Thank you, Mother."

Lunch was delicious. Even the water from the stable pump tasted sweet and cool. When they finished eating, the boys went to ask Mr. Baughman what other work he wanted them to do.

"If you are finished in the stable, all I need is for you to do some sweeping around the shop here," Mr. Baughman instructed the boys. As the boys started sweeping, five Union cavalry men rode up to the blacksmith shop.

Joseph said with a snicker to one of the men, "Are the Rebels coming again?"

The soldier ignored him. He told Mr. Baughman, "We need some new shoes for our horses. Please hurry, if you can."

"Do you have money to pay for the shoes?" the smithy asked.

"How is this?" The soldier held out a handful of coins.

"That will do," said the smithy. He started to work on one of the horses. Ben and Joseph tried to sweep as slowly as possible so that they could listen to the soldiers talk.

"I hope the rest of our troops get here before General Lee and his Rebels do," said a broken-toothed young soldier.

"Our unit could probably hold off a hundred or so Rebels, but we are licked before we even start if there are more enemy than that," a red-headed soldier responded.

"I heard that General Meade is starting to make plans to set up battle lines just west of town along Pipe Creek. Some think it will be the biggest battle yet in the war. We'll be prepared for those Rebels this time. We can't afford any more defeats like at Chancellorsville," another soldier added.

"Everything we hear is just rumors," the redhead complained. "I wouldn't mind being the first to find those Rebels. I'm sick of all these false alarms."

"Here, son," the redhead called out to Ben.

"Do you mean me, sir?" asked Ben.

"Yes, you. Here, take this penny, then brush down my horse until he is nice and shiny.

Ben looked at the penny. He was thinking that it was a joke. No one would just pay a penny for hard work. But he was surprised when Joseph jumped at the opportunity.

"Can I do someone else's horse for a penny?" Joseph asked the men.

"All right, young man." One of the other soldiers threw him a penny. Both boys looked at Mr. Baughman for permission.

"Go ahead, children. I don't have a penny to give you, and I know you can buy some good candy with all that money."

The boys brushed and curried the horses of the cavalry men

while Mr. Baughman put new shoes on them. The soldiers talked and played poker. The afternoon was hot. Flies buzzed around Ben's face and ankles. Suddenly the quiet afternoon was interrupted.

"Hands up, all of you! Don't reach for your guns or you will be shot!" The leader of a dozen of gray-coated soldiers burst into the smithy's shop and proceeded to shout more orders. "You men are under arrest. Come along quietly."

Ben stood still, unable to move, fearing that this was his last moment on earth. The Union soldiers swore but raised their hands as they had been ordered.

Joseph jumped up and down. "It's the Rebels. There's going to be a fight. Come on, men," he urged the Union soldiers. "Are you going to stand there and let those Johnnies tell you what to do?"

Ben jabbed Joseph in the ribs and said, "Hush up! Do you want to get shot or something?"

Joseph then realized that the odds were not in the bluecoats' favor. He quieted down. He said to the leader of the Rebel troop, "Are we under arrest too?"

"You boys can stay here and keep your mouths shut. It wouldn't do for anyone to go warn the other Yankees about our presence here in town. How many Union troops are there in town?" he asked Ben.

"I really don't know, sir. I just arrived here yesterday."

The leader asked each of the bluecoats, but each refused to give any information.

"I'll tell you one thing," Joseph bragged. "There are enough Union troops here in town to whup you."

The Rebels laughed. "Then I guess we better take all these pretty horses here to help us escape from these terrible Yankees," the leader said. Several of his men ran off to the stable to get horses while others rounded up their prisoners and took the horses from the blacksmith shop.

Mr. Baughman stood back against the wall. He kept his hands up, but none of the Rebels approached him because he wasn't wearing a uniform.

When Joseph saw one of the graycoats walking away with Emily, the young boy went wild. He jumped on the soldier's back and started beating him with his fists. "You can't have my horse! She's mine! Leave her alone, you traitor!"

It took two of the other soldiers to get Joseph down. They held onto him until every horse had been taken out of the shop and stable. Then they released Joseph and rode away with their prisoners.

"Let's go get them!" Joseph yelled.

Ben held onto the younger boy. "No, Joseph. Stay here where it's safe. Your mother doesn't need any more grief by having you get hurt. Remember, you are the man of the house." Ben looked around for Mr. Baughman. He was gone. "Where is Mr. Baughman?"

Joseph grinned. "He probably has sent out the alarm to the rest of the Union troops. I'm going outside to see."

Annelle Woggon Ratcliffe 1/90

Joseph didn't wait for Ben. He ran across Main Street and up Washington Road, which angled off Main towards the nation's capital. Ben was close on Joseph's heels. He could see the Rebels disappearing over a hill. The boys stood there a few minutes, trying to decide what to do next. All of a sudden, Ben heard the sound of many horses. Then he and Joseph saw a larger group of Rebels, two or three dozen, coming back over the hill.

"Here they come again!" Joseph exclaimed.

"We'd better get out of here!" Ben warned.

But from behind them came the pounding of more horses. Ben grabbed Joseph and pulled him out of the way just in time. A detachment of Union cavalrymen charged up Washington Road, sabers drawn and ready for battle. They whooped and hollered, trying to look and sound fearsome.

The boys pressed themselves against the building they were near. Soon they were joined by other curious townsfolk. The Rebels, not sure of how many other Union troops might be following this first group, tried to turn their horses around and retreat. But there wasn't enough room in the narrow street to have an orderly escape. There was much confusion. The Union soldiers took the chance to attack.

Guns started firing, sabers were swinging, men were shouting, and women were screaming. Ben covered Joseph's eyes with his hands. Joseph tried pulling them away, but with little success. When he did get a peek, he saw a horse get shot, so he helped Ben by covering his own eyes. Ben saw that the Union troops had the clear advantage and were winning. Just then, he saw something beyond the fighting men.

"Look!" he shouted to Joseph as he pointed south. There

came an endless gray column of more Rebel cavalrymen. The Union men didn't seem to care that they were quickly becoming out-numbered. Most were captured by the Rebels. Several men and a horse lay on the ground. The battle had only lasted a few minutes, but that was a few minutes too many for Ben.

Rebel troops poured into town. Joseph shouted, "Quick, we have to go home and make sure mother is all right! If any one tries to hurt her, he will be the sorriest person in the world!"

They raced among the crowds of spectators. Joseph called to his mother as soon as he entered his back yard. A few Confederate soldiers rode up the alley, slowing down when they were near the boys. Mother stepped out on the back porch at that moment. The soldiers fired their guns up into the sky, trying to scare the boys. Joseph looked at his mother and then turned towards the soldiers. He ran over to one of their horses and smacked him on the flank. The horse reared. "Get out of here, you low down scum!" he screamed at the soldier.

"Ya, scram!" Ben added.

The soldiers burst out laughing, then rode on.

"Boys come into the house right now!" Mrs. Harner ordered. Once she got the boys safely inside, she rushed around the house bolting doors, locking windows, and drawing curtains. The boys helped with the upstairs windows. Then the three sat down on Mrs. Harner's bed. Joseph and Ben told her about the battle.

A tear rolled down Joseph's mother's face. "I have tried so hard to protect you from such evil in the world. But today, I think you have seen humanity at its worst."

Suddenly, there came a loud rapping at the front door. Mrs.

Harner grabbed the boys. "Shush, quiet. Maybe they will think no one is home," she told them.

Then the knocking became more determined. Joseph peeked out between the curtains. Ben looked out the other window. There were a few Confederate soldiers at the door. He could see that many more soldiers were at the neighbors' doors too. Some were being let into homes with a warm welcome. Those were the homes of the southern sympathizers. He could see a few townsfolk having guns pointed at them for not cooperating in letting the soldiers in. Mother saw this too as she stood behind Joseph, looking over his head.

One of the soldiers at their door looked up and saw the curious eyes before Mrs. Harner could close the drapes. "I know you're in there. I'll count to five," he warned. "If you don't open up by then, I'll blast the door open with my cannon." He winked at one of his buddies.

Mrs. Harner stuck her head out the window and pleaded, "Stop! Please, stop! I'll open the door."

The men stopped pounding. One said more kindly, "We don't mean ya no harm, mam. We just need some vittles to fill our innards and water to wet our whistles."

Mrs. Harner ordered the boys to stay in the bedroom and lock the door behind her as she went down to open the front door. When he heard her go down the stairs, Joseph slowly and quietly unlocked the bedroom door.

"What are you doing?" Ben asked. "Your mother told us to stay here."

"I can't let her face those soldiers alone. If she needs me, I have to be there. Come on. We can watch from the top of the stairway without being seen."

The boys went down on their hands and knees and inched their way forward to the stairway landing. They were able to see Mrs. Harner opening the front door. The soldiers, six of them, entered. They took their hats off politely as they walked in.

One soldier, who appeared to be the youngest, said to Joseph's mother, "Mam, my name is Nathan Smith. We need food and a place to rest for an hour or two. We haven't had a square meal in weeks." He showed her his belt. Ben could see that there were many new holes punched into it where he had needed to make the belt smaller to fit his shrinking belly.

"All right, you may sit at our dining table. But I am only letting you because some day my son, who is in the Union army, may need help from one of your mothers."

She instructed the men to wash their hands and faces at the backyard pump. While they did, she set out some of the fresh bread. She fried some bacon and scrambled a basket full of eggs. As the men ate, she stood quietly over them. As each ate his fill, he started remembering his manners. Soon, they were all sitting up straighter, using their napkins, and speaking to one another in civilized conversation. It was then that Mrs. Harner walked over to the stairway. "All right, boys. I know you are there. Come on down and help me clean up." Ben and Joseph blushed as they obediently descended the stairs.

"Well, looky here," the oldest soldier, who had a long black beard, said. "You had some strong soldiers upstairs waiting to ambush us." He said to his buddies, "Watch out, men! We don't have a chance!'' He broke out in belly shaking laughs. The other soldiers joined in. The boys' faces turned brighter red.

"Tell me, son," the bearded man said to Ben, "Where do you keep your horses?"

Ben replied, "Sir, I don't have a horse. I wish I did, though."

Joseph didn't wait for the soldier to ask him. He turned to his mother and announced, "Mother, these are some of the rats that stole Emily." He then glared at the soldiers.

"Is that true?" Mrs. Harner asked the men.

Nathan said, "I don't know if any of us have your horse. I'm sorry if your horse was taken, though. About a third of our cavalry men are without horses. Many of our own horses were shot during battle or went lame. Now we need to take horses from wherever we can find them if we are to remain an army."

"That's stealing!" Joseph stated.

"You are right," the soldier responded quietly. "I feel very sorry that things have gotten so bad that we have to steal. We just got paid this week. I can offer you a few dollars. Would that help?" He held out some crinkled Confederate money. Ben had never seen that kind of money before.

"That money won't do you any good around here. Confederate money is worthless," Joseph declared.

The bearded soldier grinned. "That all depends upon who wins this here war, doesn't it? Considering we are here, only 40 miles from your capital, it looks like you just might need some of this Confederate money."

Mrs. Harner wouldn't take the money. She cleared the table. Then the soldiers sprawled out around the parlor on the sofa and the floor. Each tried to take a nap. Ben and Joseph quietly cleaned the dishes while Mrs. Harner straightened up the dining room. After about an hour, one of the soldiers woke the others. They gathered their gear together.

"Mam, we thank you for the fine food," said Nathan. The other soldiers agreed. "Horace, here, would be happy to chop some wood for you, to show our gratitude." He pointed to a strong looking man. "The rest of us will be out front feeding our horses."

Joseph's mother consented. The boys ran out to the back yard to watch the wood chopping. Then they walked up the alley. They saw that almost every house had soldiers spread out on lawns, resting. Some families were arguing with soldiers, trying to keep the men from taking their horses. The soldiers always won those arguments. Ben clearly noted that no soldier was in Mr. Flint's yard. He was certain that no one wanted to contend with Butch.

A few houses down, the boys could hear joyous singing accompanied by a piano. It was a party. Joseph explained that this was Mary O'Neil's house. Her parents were southern sympathizers. Mary saw the boys and ran out to her back fence to talk.

"See?" she boasted. "I told you we were going to win the war. We have the general of the cavalry staying at our house. His name is J.E.B. Stuart." She stuck her tongue out at Joseph and ran back into her house.

The boys did not respond to her. Joseph explained to Ben, "Mary is the neighborhood pest." Ben shook his head up and down in immediate understanding. Continuing on their walk, they reached the Catholic Church. There, a burial was taking place. Joseph tapped a nearby priest on the shoulder and whispered, "Who died?"

The priest looked solemnly down at him. "Two Confederate soldiers and two Union soldiers were killed in the battle this afternoon. They will be buried side by side, each of them being equal in the eyes of God. Rest their souls."

"Let's get out of here," Ben pleaded. "This gives me the creeps." They ran back to Joseph's house.

The soldiers were sitting on the front steps. They moved aside to let the boys into the house. Then they sat back down to continue shining their guns. Ben, Joseph, and his mother ate what food was left over. A gentle knock was heard at the front door. Mrs. Harner answered it. There stood Nathan.

"We are leaving now, Mrs. Harner. Thank you again for your courtesy. I hope both your sons will be safe throughout the war."

"Thank you," she responded. She and the boys watched as the Rebels rode away. She sighed, "I pray to God that none of the men I helped tries to kill Andrew."

Soldiers were leaving from all of the houses. The streets became very quiet after the cavalry left. Mrs. Harner sent the boys to bed even though it was not dark yet.

CHAPTER 4

TUESDAY, JUNE 30*th*, 1863

Bang! Bang! Bang, bang, bang!

Ben and Joseph sat up in bed. It was morning. Gunshots rang through the streets outside. Ben could feel the hair standing up on the back of his neck.

"Now what's happening?" Ben asked Joseph.

Joseph shrugged his shoulders. Then they heard a growing sound of horses galloping down Main Street. Soon they could hear the voices of men, possibly hundreds of them, filling the streets.

"I thought all the soldiers left last night," Ben said.

Ben and Joseph hopped out of bed and ran to the window. "Hooray!" he shouted. It's our troops. I hope they'll catch up to those Rebels and show them a thing or two. Maybe they'll even get Emily back for me." He ran to wake up his mother, but she was already awake and dressed. There came a knocking on the front door just like the day before.

"Here we go again," said Mrs. Harner. "I'll let them in while you boys get dressed. As soon as you are ready, come down and help me."

This time there were about twelve soldiers at the door. The streets were flooded with blue-coated men and their horses. Before the men at her door could say anything, Mrs. Harner announced, "Welcome to my home. I assume you are here to get food." The men nodded in agreement. She continued, "I must apologize for being short on food, but the Rebels ate almost everything I had in the pantry."

One of the soldiers spoke up. "My name is John Ray and this is my brother, David." He pointed to a man who looked so much like himself that they must have been twins. "These other men are our friends. We would be grateful to you for any food you could give us."

Ben and Joseph had been spying on the soldiers, hoping Mrs. Harner wouldn't notice. Ben stared long and hard at the Rays. They could not have been more than 17 or 18 years old, but there was a tired air about them that made them look, in some ways, like old men who had seen more trouble than any man should have to see.

Mrs. Harner also saw that look. She said cheerfully, "How about some griddle cakes. I have some flour and eggs left." The men grinned. That brought a more youthful look back into the Ray boys' faces.

"That sounds just fine, madam," John answered for the group.

So, as on the day before, Mrs. Harner went into the kitchen to cook. The boys brought load after load of griddle cakes out to the hungry men. Ben whispered to Joseph, "How often do you folks have to feed soldiers like this?"

Joseph responded, "Before this week, we have never had to feed soldiers. We haven't seen more than a few dozen soldiers in this town before now. All this activity must prove that there is going to be a big battle soon."

When the soldiers finished their food, Ben approached David. "Excuse me, but could you tell me why so many soldiers are coming through Westminster?"

"All I know is that we've been sent to stop the Rebels from invading Washington and Baltimore."

Suddenly, Ben realized what was happening. He said to Joseph, "I'll bet they are going to Gettysburg."

"What makes you say that?" asked Joseph.

"Are you kidding?" asked Ben. "That was where the most famous battle of the Civil War took place."

One of the soldiers overheard Ben. "What are you talking about, son. Do you have some secret information that we should know?"

"Uh, no, sir. I mean, it just seems that most of the soldiers are heading north, and Gettysburg is the only town north of here that I know." Ben's hands got cold and clammy.

The soldier stared at Ben for a minute and then turned back to talk to his friends. Joseph pulled Ben out into the parlor.

"It's a good thing that you didn't get into bigger trouble. I don't know how we would ever be able to explain who you are and why you know the things you do."

"I'm sorry I said anything, but listen, you don't realize what is happening here!" Ben exclaimed. He spoke quickly with excitement. "I'm not sure which day or which year it is actually supposed to happen, but an incredibly large battle took place at Gettysburg. Thousands and thousands of men were killed. That was the battle that determined the outcome of the whole war."

Joseph listened with interest.

"My parents took me to Gettysburg when we first moved here. There is a huge graveyard there where dead soldiers from the battle were buried. Along some of the roads, old Civil War cannons have been set up for people to look at. The cannons don't really work anymore, but they still look scary and dangerous when you get real close to one. I sure wouldn't want one of those aimed at my body."

"Why would the battle take place in Gettysburg?" Joseph asked. "It's just a little farming town like Westminster. It has no special value to the North or to the South."

"I heard a tour guide say that the battle happened in Gettysburg because several important roads come together there. I guess it was a good meeting place for all the troops that had been scattered over Maryland and Pennsylvania."

Joseph thought for a moment. "If you're right, then there is nothing we can do about it. I guess I will just have to be glad that the battle will not be any closer to home. I don't want to see anything worse than what we saw yesterday.''

Soon the soldiers stood up. They thanked Mrs. Harner and left. She had given them directions to stores in town where they could buy new boots and other supplies. She and the boys ate their own breakfast. It took almost an hour to wash all the dishes and clean up the kitchen and dining room.

Another knock was heard at the front door. In exasperation Mrs. Harner shouted through the closed door, "We're out of food!" But the soldier at the door opened it without an invitation to enter. A tall, broad-shouldered young soldier stood in the doorway. He wore a saber on his left hip.

Ben gasped. Was this soldier going to attack them? He turned to run but stopped when he saw Joseph. The young boy was running toward the soldier. *Oh, my gosh, Joseph is sure to get shot,* Ben thought. He shouted, "Stop!", just as Joseph jumped into the arms of the soldier and gave him a bear hug.

Mrs. Harner just looked stunned. She didn't move while she watched Joseph and the soldier. Tears rolled down her cheeks. Then she walked toward the soldier and said, "Andrew, oh, Andrew. Thank God you have come home to me." She held out her arms. Her elder son came to her and hugged her with Joseph sandwiched in between them.

Ben started to feel like he was in the way. This was apparently Joseph's older brother. The family might want to be alone right now. But Joseph proceeded to introduce Andrew to Ben. Andrew smiled and shook hands with Ben. Then the family started talking to each other again.

"What brings you home, son?" Mrs. Harner asked. "I didn't expect you until next Christmas."

"I'm here with my company. I received permission from Brigadier General Custer to stop at home for a few minutes. We have been chasing the tail end of a Confederate cavalry unit," Andrew explained.

"They were here yesterday," Joseph announced. "They stole Emily."

"I'm sorry to hear that," Andrew said to Joseph as he set him down and put his big hand on Joseph's shoulder. He laid the rifle down with his other hand. "I know you loved that horse. But, to tell you the truth, the horse I am riding, I had to take from a family too. My horse went lame. I needed to keep up with my company or I might have been captured. So I took a horse. I guess we're even now. If I still have this new horse when the war is over, I will bring him home to you."

"How long can you stay?" asked Mrs. Harner.

"About fifteen minutes. We are heading north. Most of the Army of the Potomac has received orders to find General Lee's army."

"Then sit down and have a cup of coffee and some griddle cakes. Between bites, you can tell us how you are doing," his mother directed. She made Andrew comfortable and then sat down to talk with him. Ben did not listen much to the conversation. He was deep in thought. He began to get nervous and fidgety.

Joseph whispered to him, "What is your problem?"

Ben leaned over and whispered in Joseph's ear, "I need to speak to you in private. It's very important."

Joseph let out a frustrated sigh and said to his family, "Excuse us, please. We'll be right back." Mrs. Harner and Andrew kept talking, knowing they had so little time together.

Ben pulled Joseph into the kitchen. "We can't let Andrew ride with Custer to Gettysburg. If this is the same Custer I am thinking of, there is a really good chance that your brother will be killed in the battle at Gettysburg!"

Joseph turned pale. "What makes you say that?" he demanded.

"Your brother mentioned Custer."

"You mean Brigadier General Custer?" Joseph asked.

"Yes. Is his first name George?"

"Yes. Andrew wrote that name in a letter he sent us. How did you know?"

"General George Custer is very famous in history. He was well known for having no fear of the enemy in battle. But that lack of fear caused him to lead his men into many dangerous situations. Eventually, he was killed along with all of his men in the Battle at Little Big Horn soon after the war.

Joseph started to act panicky. "Do you really think Andrew is in serious danger?"

"Yes, I do."

"What can we do?" Joseph pleaded with Ben. "We can't tell him what you told me. He would just laugh at us. We only have about ten minutes to do something."

"We will have to hold him here for longer than that. We have to figure out a way to keep him from leaving. Can you think of any way we can tie him up, or something like that, without your mother stopping us?" Ben asked.

"Let me think a minute," said Joseph. He tried to calm himself down so that his brain would work. Finally he said, "I have it!" If we can get him to the outhouse, we can lock him in it without Mother catching us."

"Don't you think she would get suspicious?" Ben asked.

"Not if we tell her that Andrew has gone on with his men because he was too sad to have to say 'goodbye' to her again."

"Brilliant!" said Ben. "Now, how should we lure him to the outhouse?"

Joseph thought again. "Let's try having him drink a lot of coffee. That will fill him so full of liquid that he will have to use the outhouse or burst. When he goes in, we will nail the door shut. There are boards lying out behind the outhouse. A hammer and nails are on the back porch."

"Good. I'll go outside and wait. I'll get the hammer and nails and hide behind the outhouse. Tell them that I went home to see if my parents are there yet." Ben went out the kitchen door. Joseph returned to the dining room. No one asked about Ben.

Joseph picked up the pot of coffee. "Here, Andrew, let me fill up your cup with more coffee." Joseph poured it before Andrew could stop him.

Andrew drank the coffee quickly so that he could continue talking with his mother. As soon as the cup was empty, Joseph filled it up again. Not wanting to hurt his little brother's feelings, Andrew drank a little bit of the coffee at a time, but rested his hand on the top of his cup when he wasn't drinking so that Joseph wouldn't fill it up again.

Soon it was time for Andrew to leave. "Excuse me, Mother," he said, "I have to go soon. But first, I will run out to the back yard for a moment. When I come back, I will give you your kiss." He stood up and walked out through the kitchen. Joseph knew where he was going and followed him.

"I think I can do this by myself, little brother," Andrew laughed.

"Yes, I know, but I just want to be near you as long as possible," Joseph responded. When they got to the outhouse, Joseph said, "I'll wait for you out here."

"Suit yourself," said Andrew as he entered and closed the door.

Quickly, Ben popped out from behind the shack. He quietly handed Joseph a board. Joseph held it in place while Ben held the hammer in his right hand and positioned the nail with the other. "Bam, bam, bam!" One nail was in.

"Hey, what's going on out there?" yelled Andrew.

"Sorry," Joseph responded. "I'm just throwing rocks at the side of the outhouse while I'm waiting."

"Bam, bam, bam!" The other side of the board was nailed into place.

"That doesn't sound like rocks to me!" called Andrew. "That sounds more like a hammer. I'll be right out."

"Bam, bam, 'ouch', bam!" One side of a second board was in place. As Ben sucked at his bruised thumb, Joseph said to Andrew, "No need to hurry. I'll stop making noise." Ben went ahead and nailed the last side of the board.

"Darn, you. I'm coming out." Andrew tried to open the door. He wasn't able to budge it. "Hey, let me out of here right now!" he shouted.

"I'm sorry." Joseph explained, "I can't let you out. If I do, you will get killed."

"No, I won't! Let me out of here!" Andrew shouted.

Joseph started crying. "Yes, you will. I can't tell you how I know, but you will." Ben stood next to Joseph, not sure if he should say anything or not. He put his hand gently onto Joseph's shaking shoulder.

No voice came from the outhouse for a few seconds. Then Andrew said, "Joseph, if I don't go back to my company, it will be much more likely that I will get shot by a firing squad for deserting the army. I must go, now!"

"No! No! I can't let you!" Joseph wailed.

Joseph's mother came out into the back yard. "What is taking you two so long?" she asked. Then she saw Joseph crying and asked, "What's wrong, son?"

The voice from inside the outhouse called out, "Mother, tell Joseph to let me out of here!"

She saw the barricaded door. Then she seemed to understand why Joseph was crying and what he had done. "Joseph, I know you love your brother and you want him to stay with us, but you must let him go immediately. If you don't, then I will have to take the boards off myself."

"Mother," Joseph sobbed, "you don't understand!"

Mrs. Harner took the hammer from Ben. As she tried to pry away the two boards that were sealing Andrew in the outhouse, Ben said, "I was just trying to help."

"I know, Ben. But this is not the way to help." She slowly worked each board off.

Andrew stepped out. He went over to Joseph, leaned down, and kissed him. "I'm not angry with you. I promise to be very careful for the rest of the war. You can see that I've made it this long already without getting hurt. I love you and Mother very much, and I plan to come back to you."

Joseph hugged Andrew as if it were the last time he would ever see him. He wrapped himself around Andrew like an octopus as Andrew walked back toward the house. Back in the parlor, Andrew kissed his mother and shook hands with Ben. Then he peeled Joseph off and said, "Be brave, little brother. I don't want you getting Mother worried about me."

Joseph stood up straight and sniffed back his sobs. Out in the street, Andrew untied his horse from the hitching post and climbed into the saddle. A few of his fellow soldiers joined him. They all started riding down Main Street toward the road to Gettysburg.

Suddenly, a piercing screech broke out from Mary O'Neil's

upstairs window. Mary was screaming to the soldiers at the top of her lungs, "Get out of here, you dirty Yankees!" Ben and Joseph saw her raise a sling shot and aim it at the soldiers. She shot a rock. It hit Andrew's horse on the behind. The horse whinnied. As it reared up, Andrew was thrown to the ground. A loud groan came from Andrew's mouth as his face twisted in pain. He grabbed his left ankle as he rocked back and forth on the ground.

Mrs. Harner ran to her son. She made him lie still as she gently tried to remove his boot. Even that gentle touch was too painful for his ankle. Mrs. Harner had one of the soldiers cut a slit down one side of the boot with a pocket knife. Then the boot just fell off. When she examined the ankle, she found that it was indeed broken. Andrew's friends carried him back into his house. One of the soldiers was instructed to let Brigadier General Custer know what happened to Andrew and to request permission for him to stay at home until the ankle improved.

Joseph looked very worried about his brother being in such pain. Ben reminded him, "Joseph, cheer up. Now Andrew doesn't have to go to Gettysburg. He is not going to die from a broken ankle!" Joseph looked at Ben, then broke out in a huge smile.

Andrew's mother arranged the parlor sofa as a make-shift hospital bed for Andrew. The soldiers carefully set him down on the sofa. She propped his foot up on a pillow. Mrs. Harner finished cutting away the whole front of the boot so that Andrew's foot could easily be placed in the L-shaped remains, forming a splint. Then she loosely wrapped bandages around the boot and foot together to hold it in place.

The rest of the afternoon was spent turning the house into a hospital for Andrew. Ben and Joseph became tired of running little errands for Andrew, but they didn't complain. Each time they had to run outside for something, Ben noticed that more and more covered wagons and soldiers were pouring into town. A messenger brought a note to Mrs. Harner from Custer. He gave permission for Andrew to stay at home until he could be moved to a military hospital.

After supper, Joseph asked Andrew to tell Ben and him a story. He did.

Let me tell you the story of Mighty Lloyd Logan. I met the man right after the Battle of Bull Run last year. Now, you remember that the North lost that battle. When we rode away from that one, we were a mighty sorry looking group. None of us would speak. Two days after the fight, we were camping on a mountainside near a stream that was bordered by a thick forest of oak trees. All I could hear was the sound of the stream and the singing of birds and crickets. It was the first peaceful moment we had for weeks.

Just as I lay my head down on my bedroll to sleep, I heard the fiercest yowling sound I had ever heard echo throughout the woods. Every man in my company sat up, looking at each other, wondering if the other knew what the sound was. The sound continued, coming closer and closer. Now it was starting to sound more like a growl of of some wild animal. Suddenly, a large beast rushed out of the woods.

"What was it?" asked Joseph.

"I bet it was a bear," Ben stated.

"No. It was Lloyd Logan." Andrew continued with his story.

Lloyd was a huge man. He stood about six foot four and must have weighed about 250 pounds. He had curly black hair covering his scalp, chin, and chest. His arms were as big around as my legs and his legs were as big around as my waist. He was sure lucky that none us put a bullet through him. Fortunately, we were all too stunned to think of our guns.

"I'm here to join up with you," he announced. "Where is my horse?"

"You can't stay with us. Get out of here," my friend Lawrence said to Lloyd.

But Lloyd wouldn't leave. He said, "My paw told me there was cavalry headed this way. I sure am glad I found you. My family has never been able to buy a horse before. Paw said that if I joined up with the cavalry, you would give me a horse. After the war I could bring the horse back to the farm."

"Do you know how to ride?" I asked him.

"I ain't never tried to ride a horse before, but I can ride a mule. I can do anything I put my mind to doin'. Just give me a horse and I'll show you I can ride him."

My friends and I had a feeling that this mountain man would never make a good cavalry man, but we thought we would tease him a little, just for fun. Lloyd looked like he would be very strong, so we thought of getting him to do some of our work for us.

Lawrence said, "We might consider letting you join

up, but right now we need to make a campfire and find
something to eat. You get the firewood and we will get
the food out.''

"I'll build you the best darn fire you ever saw,''
Lloyd responded with a big smile. We saw him disappear
into the woods. The rest of us took our dried beef jerky
and coffee beans from our back packs. We could hear
wood being chopped deep in the forest.

We expected to see Lloyd come out into the clearing with an armload of firewood. Instead, he walked
towards us dragging a whole tree. As we stared with our
mouths hanging open, Lloyd swung his ax over and over
again, first chopping the branches off the tree, then cutting the trunk into sections. He split the sections into
firewood. In less than an hour, he had a huge fire blaz-
ing. None of us had ever seen anyone work so fast and
with such strength.

"So,'' said Lloyd Logan, "where's the meat you
want to cook?''

I handed him my beef jerky.

"You call this meat?'' Lloyd asked me.

"That's all I have,'' I told him.

"Well why didn't you say so?'' he laughed. "I'll get
some real meat for you if you loan me your gun for a
few minutes.

I handed my rifle to him. He stood in the middle
of the camp and turned slowly around, gazing with pierc-

ing eyes into the surrounding woods. There was a small clearing in one direction. As he stared in that direction he quietly asked me, "Do you like ham?"

"Sure," I said.

He shot the rifle. Then he ran to the far end of the moonlit clearing. It must have been 100 yards away. I swear that none of us had seen any animal in that direction, but sure enough, he came walking back with a wild boar in his arms. He butchered it right there and we roasted the meat. We all ate like kings that night.

"Now can I have a horse?" Lloyd asked me after he was done eating.

"Let me talk with my men first," I said. We soldiers huddled together to talk. Lloyd waited on the other side of the campsite. I said to my friends, "If he can ride even half as well as he shoots, I sure wouldn't mind having him join us."

"Heck," said Christopher Gunther, "even if he can't ride a hoot, I wouldn't mind having him with us. I bet he could pick off the enemy from a mile away. Besides, we would never go hungry with him around."

We all voted. It was unanimous. We all wanted Lloyd.

I went up to him and held out my hand to shake his. "Lloyd, we would be proud to have you join up with us. Welcome to the Union Army."

Lloyd dropped his hand. He had a look of shock on his face. "Did you say the Union Army?" he asked.

Annelle Woggon Ratcliffe 1/90

"Of course," I said.

"Well, dog gone it!" Lloyd complained. He picked up his ax and started to walk away.

"Where are you going?" I asked. "What's wrong?"

"I ain't joining no Union Army. I thought you was the Rebs. My daddy would whup me good if I joined up with you Yankees." He walked off into the woods and we never saw him again. But we had many a good laugh after that trying to imagine anyone trying to spank Mighty Lloyd Logan.

"Do you think he ever joined up with the Rebels?" Ben asked Andrew.

"There's no telling. I figure that if we were the first soldiers he had seen in the first two years of the war, he probably wouldn't see any more for another year or so.

"Tell us another story," Joseph said.

Mrs. Harner came into the parlor just then. "Off to bed, young men. Let Andrew rest now."

CHAPTER 5

WEDNESDAY JULY 1*st*, 1863

The noise outside the bedroom window did not waken the boys. They were becoming used to the constant rumbling of countless wagons. Mrs. Harner had to come into the room to get the boys out of bed. She pulled the covers off each, then opened the curtains to let in the morning light. "Time to get up, boys!" she ordered.

Ben stretched and sat up sleepily. Joseph reached down and pulled the sheet back over his head.

"Stay in bed if you like," his mother told him, "but you won't get any of the strawberry preserves and fresh biscuits I just baked."

Joseph popped right up. The boys could smell the aroma of steaming hot biscuits. "We'll be down in a minute, Mother."

The boys pulled on their britches and slid down the stairway banister. Andrew was still in the parlor. He was already eating his biscuits. Joseph smiled at him and called out a happy, "Hello." Jokingly, Joseph said to Ben, "We better hurry up and have our breakfast before Andrew eats it all."

Andrew just smiled and kept on eating. He was clearly so thankful to have good food to eat that he didn't want to waste time talking.

Ben and Joseph ate their breakfast in the kitchen. Afterwards, they helped Mrs. Harner care for Andrew. They brought warm water in a bowl so Andrew could wash his face and hands. Then Mrs. Harner inspected Andrew's ankle again.

"I don't believe we will be able to bandage the ankle any better than this until the swelling goes down. Then we can get a good cast on it," she said.

"Mother, may Ben and I walk down to his house to see if his parents are home, yet?" Joseph asked. Ben was surprised at the question.

"I wish you would," she answered. "I'm getting worried that something might have happened to them. They should have been home by now."

Joseph led Ben out the front door.

"What's up?" asked Ben.

"Look around you!" Joseph demanded.

Ben did. The streets were completely filled with covered wagons moving slowly towards the middle of town. Soldiers were crowding the sidewalks. There was almost no room for the boys to walk.

"Come on, Ben!" Joseph urged Ben. "This town has never seen so much excitement. I want to see what everyone is doing before it's too late. Who knows if the soldiers will still be here tomorrow?"

As they approached the general store, Joseph said, "Let's stop here first to buy some candy with the money we earned at the stable." But the entrance to the store was blocked with soldiers trying to enter to buy supplies. The boys were glad that they were small enough to squeeze among the men to get to the candy shelf. Mr. Shriver, the grown son of the store's owner, saw the boys, but he was too busy to help them.

"Need me to help you, Mr. Shriver?" Joseph called over to the busy man. Mr. Shriver nodded his head up and down. "This will be fun," Joseph said to Ben. "I have helped Mr. Shriver many times."

The boys came around to the other side of the counter. They were instantly bombarded with requests by soldiers for help. Joseph would get the item requested, tell Ben the price, and Ben would take the money from the soldier and give the correct change. Most of the soldiers were trying to buy boots, belts, suspenders, and other practical supplies. But others were buying souvenirs, like ribbons and jewelry, to sent home to their loved ones. Within two hours, the store was sold out of boots. The soldiers began to leave to try other stores.

Mr. Shriver finally had a moment to come over and thank the boys for their help. "Thanks to you boys, I sold more today than I have in the past two months. Each of you may take a small bag and fill it with whatever candy you like. You may also each take a half-dime from the cash box." Mr. Shriver knew Joseph's two favorite things were candy and money.

Ben whispered to Joseph, "How are we going to break a dime in half? Can't he give us each a nickel?"

"I'm not sure what a nickel is, but here is your half-dime," Joseph said.

Ben looked closely at it. It was a silvery coin like a dime, but slightly smaller. On one side, it had an engraving of a lady. She was wearing a long, flowing gown and she was sitting on a stool or chair. On the other side, the words 'half dime' were engraved. Ben realized that he had been giving some of the soldiers the wrong change all afternoon, thinking the coins were dimes. "Oops," he said softly to himself.

"Thank you, sir," Joseph said. He handed Ben a bag and took one for himself. Ben chose peppermint sticks, rock candy, and lemon drops. He didn't pay much attention to Joseph's choices. They both waved goodbye to Mr. Shriver, then went out on the back step of the store to eat the candy in peace and quiet.

Two soldiers walked into the alley where the boys sat. As they strolled, they were in deep conversation. The boys were ignored, so it was easy to overhear what the soldiers said.

"Did you hear the cannons on your way into town this morning?" the fat soldier said to the freckled one.

"Sure did. Can't hear it in town with all the noise of the people and wagons, but where it's quiet in the countryside, I could tell the big battle must be under way."

Ben and Joseph looked at each other in surprise. Ben wondered what all the soldiers were doing here in Westminster if the battle was north of here.

"I hate being ordered here to guard the supply wagons and railroad when most of the other men can go to Gettysburg to fight. What will I tell my grandchildren when I am old?" the fat one said.

"I'm more worried about what my girl will say. She'll probably think I wasn't brave enough to fight. It's hard for her to understand that I can't choose where I go or what I do," the freckled soldier replied.

Ben whispered to Joseph, "They don't know how lucky they are to miss this battle."

Joseph called out to the men, "Did you men say that a battle has started?"

The fat soldier frowned at Joseph, probably thinking that children should be seen and not heard. But the freckled soldier was younger and eager to show his greater knowledge to the boys.

"A big battle in Gettysburg started last night. Lee's troops, thousands of them, met up with some of our troops. The generals figured that Gettysburg was as good a place as any to stage the battle that both sides have been preparing for over the past few weeks. Now there is a big rush for as many Union troops as possible to get to Gettysburg to stop Lee."

"Then why are you men still here?" Joseph asked. "There must be hundreds of you just walking around town."

The fat soldier held his head up proudly. "Can't fight a battle without supplies, can you?" Joseph and Ben shook their heads. "How do you think soldiers get the ammunition they need for a big fight? Each man can only carry enough bullets to last him an hour or so. What if a rifle breaks? What about bandages and medicine for the wounded soldiers? Can't do without supplies. That's why we're here. We are helping to guard these supply wagons, hundreds of them. Supplies come from Baltimore to Westminster by train. Our wagons are loaded to carry the supplies to Gettysburg. The Rebs may try to blow up the railroad or rob the wagons, but we won't let them.''

The two soldiers turned from the boys and walked off looking much more pleased with themselves than when the boys first saw them.

"That gives me an idea," said Joseph. "I would love to go outside of town and hear some of the battle sounds, wouldn't you?"

"I'm not too sure," Ben responded.

"I won't let you get hurt," Joseph laughed. "My Uncle Abe lives just north of town along the road to Gettysburg. We could go visit him today if my mother says it is all right."

"But I can't leave here."

"Why?" asked Joseph.

"I have to stay here and try to get home."

"But this is a chance in a lifetime," Joseph urged. "I promise I'll bring you back to Westminster tomorrow."

"I'm sorry, Joseph, but I can't afford to miss any chance there might be to get back into my house."

"But what if you climb back through the window and it doesn't take you back to your own time?"

Ben's eyes opened wide. He hadn't thought about that. *If going back through that window doesn't work, then I'm probably stuck here forever. I would never see Mom and Dad again. I would have no place to live. I'd be on my own with no money. Maybe I should put off trying to get back into the house until I figure out what I would do if I'm here to stay.*

Ben said to Joseph, "Maybe it wouldn't hurt to leave town for just a little while. How would we get to your uncle's house?"

"Look at all these wagons going in that direction. We could try to catch a ride on one of them," Joseph suggested.

"Do you think your uncle would mind if I came along with you?"

"No, he likes it when I bring friends along. He doesn't have any sons and he misses having boys around to help with the farm work. We could spend the night and then come home tomorrow morning. I'm sure he would give us a ride home."

Each boy stuffed his candy bag in his own shirt and ran back to Joseph's house. "Let me go in and talk to my mother. I'll tell her your parents are home now, and they gave you permission to go with me since they want you to get some farm-fresh eggs and butter for them," Joseph said to Ben.

"What will we do about lunch?" Ben asked.

"I'll pack up two lunches, and we can bring them along on the trip. Wish me luck with Mother!" Ben gave Joseph a thumbs up sign.

Ben sat down on the Harner's front step. Joseph seemed to be taking a long time. He decided to go around to the back of the house and peak in the kitchen window to see what was taking Joseph so long. Ben could hear Joseph puttering around in the kitchen. He happened to look at Mr. Flint's yard. Butch was gone. The broken window was unguarded. He started to run towards it, but then he hesitated. *What if it doesn't work? What if it doesn't work?* Ben turned away from the window, then turned back towards it. *This may be the only chance I ever get. I have to try.*

Echoes of his mother's voice ran through Ben's brain even though she wasn't there. "Now, Ben, be sure to be polite and thank your host." He realized that he should say "goodbye" to Joseph first. The little guy deserved that much. Ben raced up the Harner's back steps. He peeked in the door first to make sure Joseph was alone. He was, so Ben entered.

"Joseph, Butch is gone. I'm going to try to get home. Thank you for everything!"

Joseph looked very surprised, but said, "Sure, go ahead. I'll miss you." Then Joseph held up the bag of food, "Do you want to take your lunch with you?"

Ben smiled, "No, thanks." Ben waved and ran back out the door. He hopped over the fence and ran to the broken window.

Suddenly, Mr. Flint's back door opened. The bad-tempered man shouted, "Get out of here! I knew I couldn't trust you!"

Ben crouched low in an attempt to avoid Mr. Flint's attack and to try to enter his window, but he wasn't quick enough. Butch came charging out of the Flint house. The big dog bit Ben's pants' leg, but fortunately had only fabric, no skin, in his teeth. Ben screamed as he dragged himself and the growling dog towards

Joseph's fence. Butch let go of Ben just long enough to let out a fierce bark. That was all the time the boy needed to jump over the fence to safety.

Joseph had heard the noise outside. He was soon at the fence to help Ben. "Keep your mangy mutt away from my friend!" Joseph shouted while shaking his fist at his neighbor.

"Only if you keep your mangy bodies off my property!" Mr. Flint yelled back before he went back into his house. Butch remained outside.

Mrs. Harner came out onto the back porch. "What is all the ruckus?"

"Butch got a hold of Ben, but everything is all right now," Joseph explained.

"Are you hurt, Ben?" she asked. Ben reassured her that he was not hurt. Then she said, "I was so happy to hear from Joseph that your parents are home safely. You will enjoy your trip to Uncle Abe's. You tell him that I say to give you the best eggs he has. Have a good trip." She handed Joseph the bag of food. "Don't forget to thank Mr. Leeds for the ride to Uncle Abe's and be a good boy," she said and kissed him on the head. Ben stared at Joseph when he realized Joseph had lied to her again.

"Aw, Mother!" Joseph said with embarrassment. He and Ben walked through the house to say "goodbye" to Andrew. Then they walked down Main Street toward the railroad station.

Ben was quiet. He was still upset over the dog's attack, but he was rather relieved that he and Joseph were leaving town. He didn't want to see Butch or Mr. Flint again for a long time.

Joseph broke the silence between them, "Almost got your leg chomped off, didn't you?"

"That was too close," Ben said. He looked downward. "I guess I'll never see my family again."

"I don't believe that," Joseph stated. "Next time you have a chance to climb through the window, you don't have to stop to say 'goodbye'. I will understand and I'll be happy for you. All right?"

"All right," Ben responded.

The Western Maryland Railroad ran north and south through the middle of town. As the boys neared the depot, they found it more and more difficult to push their way through the crowds of soldiers. Heavy supply wagons slowly rumbled in line up to the train station platform. Soldiers unloaded the train cars and wheeled the supplies on big push carts to the waiting wagons. Each wagon was quickly loaded and moved on so the next could be loaded.

The huge iron engine of the train caught Ben's eye. "I've seen a train engine like that at Disney World!" he exclaimed.

"Is that a world we haven't discovered yet?" Joseph asked.

"No," Ben laughed. "Disney World is just a really great amusement park. Do you think we can climb on that engine for a few minutes?"

"Let's ask the conductor," said Joseph.

The boys were twenty feet away from the engine, but were stopped by one of the soldiers. "Boys, this is a restricted area. Only

Annelle Woggon Ratcliffe 1/90

military personnel are allowed anywhere near this train. I'm surprised you got this far. Now, go home.''

Joseph thought quickly. "But the engineer is my father. I have his lunch here in this bag. My mother said that I had to bring it to him. See?'' Joseph held up the lunch bag.

The soldier looked in the bag, then he eyed the boys suspiciously. Deciding that the boys were probably too young to be spies, he let them go on the train engine.

It was a monstrous black machine with a cone-shaped smokestack. A cow-catcher jutted out in front of the engine, like a shovel, to push away any animal that might be sitting on the tracks.

The engineer was not in his cab. The boys climbed up anyway to wait and watch the soldiers work. They had a good view from that height. The longer they watched, the easier it was to identify which of the soldiers were guards and which were laborers.

"See that wagon over there?'' Ben asked Joseph. He pointed to a covered wagon that had already been loaded. It was pulled out of the long line. The driver was sitting on one of the mules that was harnessed up closest to the wagon. The man's head hung down so low that his chin rested upon his chest. His shoulders rose slowly up and down. Ben decided that the man must be sleeping.

"That's the wagon we'll take to my uncle's house,'' Joseph stated. "Look! There aren't any guards near it. That's our best chance.'' Ben agreed.

When the guards nearest to the train were not looking, the boys slipped down from the engine and quietly edged their way toward the rear of the covered wagon they had chosen. They already knew which soldiers to avoid. No guards saw them. The laborers didn't seem to notice the boys. Ben and Joseph climbed into the wagon. It was filled with wooden crates. Whoever had packed the wagon didn't want the boxes to bump against each other, so they had packed straw between them. This spacing made room for the boys to wriggle down into the straw, providing a great hiding place.

Joseph whispered to Ben. "We can jump out the back when we get near my uncle's farm."

The wagon driver suddenly gave a big snort, brushed something away from his face, and then went back to snoring peacefully. This caused Ben to start giggling. Joseph put his hand over Ben's mouth to muffle the sound, but Ben's body still shook with laughter.

"Be quiet, " Joseph whispered. "Quick, think of something sad."

Ben started thinking about his parents. His laughter stopped. Joseph quietly opened the lunch bag and handed Ben a slice of ham and two biscuits. "Let's eat while we're waiting for the wagon to roll," Joseph said.

Ben gratefully accepted the food and ate in silence. The noise of the busy soldiers outside the wagon carried to the boys. Two voices became louder than the others. Apparently the speakers were very close to the wagon.

"Did you see two boys wandering around here?" one voice asked the other.

"There was a boy who talked to me about an hour ago. He was with an older boy. The younger one said his father was the train engineer."

"I am the train engineer. I don't have a son. I saw the boys in my cab, but by the time I could run over to the train, they were gone."

"I'll keep an eye out for them, sir. But I wouldn't worry too much. They seemed pretty harmless."

"Well, I sure hope so for your sake," the engineer warned the guard.

Ben and Joseph stopped eating. Now all the guards would be looking for them. Each boy buried himself under the straw and lay still. Minutes went by. The heat was making Ben feel sleepy. He couldn't hear a single sound from Joseph's side of the wagon. Maybe the little guy had fallen asleep. Before he knew it, Ben found himself falling asleep too, and it felt wonderful.

Annelle Woggon Ratcliffe 1/90

CHAPTER 6

WEDNESDAY AFTERNOON JULY 1st, 1863

Ben felt a hard blow to his head, which woke him up. His head had bounced against the wooden floor of the wagon whose wheel had hit a large pothole in the road. He sat up and looked for Joseph. Joseph was still sleeping even though the wagon was steadily shaking with the vibrations caused by traveling along a rocky road.

"Wake up, Joseph," Ben ordered in a low voice as he shook his friend.

Joseph opened one eye. He saw Ben and then realized the wagon was moving. With both eyes wide open, he asked Ben, "How long have we been on the road?"

"I'm not sure," Ben said quietly. "I just woke up myself. I'll peek outside to see where we are." Ben crawled to the back end of the wagon. He was very careful as he attempted to look out from under the canvas flap covering the back opening to the wagon. The road dust that was churned up by the wheels of the wagon train flew into his face. He coughed and sneezed into his shirt, trying to keep the driver from hearing him. When he could speak again he told Joseph, "It looks like we are only about a mile out of town, but we are going to have to change our plans. There are dozens of covered wagons behind us. There is no way we can jump out of here without someone seeing us."

Joseph crawled to the front of the wagon to see what the view would be. The cloth covering the framework of the walls and ceiling of the wagon was gathered together in the front, leaving only a small opening for Joseph to look through. He reported back to Ben. "There are lots of wagons in front of us, too.

"What are we going to do now?" Ben asked.

"If we tried to jump now, we would probably be trampled by horses. There is nothing we can do except wait for the wagons to stop. Then we can try to slip out of the wagon and take our chances with getting caught."

The boys spent the next hour lying quietly in the straw. They would occasionally whisper to each other. As the afternoon wore on, the hot July sun heated the wagon canvas so that Ben felt like he was in an oven. He could see the wagon driver's head from where he lay. The driver frequently wiped sweat from the back of his neck with his bandanna. The man's hat had a wet stain of sweat around the edges.

Ben suggested to Joseph, "Let's move closer to the front. There may be some breeze up there." Joseph nodded his head and they both scooted forward to that they were on each side of the opening where the driver couldn't see them. A faint, dusty, but refreshing current of air reached their faces.

The Carroll County countryside was beautiful. The foothills of the Blue Ridge Mountains rolled on and on. To Ben, they looked like a soft green blanket covering the bulging curves of a sleeping giant. In the distance he could see the purple line of a mountain ridge to the west. The wagon moved past wheat fields, corn fields, and orchards.

Joseph pulled a string from his pocket and prepared it to play "cat's cradle". Ben played with him. Suddenly, the wagon wheels made a different sound. Instead of the rattling sound of wheels on stones, Ben heard the rumbling and clunking of wooden wheels on hollow sounding boards. He peeked outside.

They were crossing a bridge over a winding creek. To the right was a large brick building on the edge of the creek. The structure was three stories high. It had more than a dozen windows lined up in neat rows. In front of the building that looked like a factory, there was a sprawling wooden house. It looked big enough to cover half a city block. Ben had seen those buildings before. It was the Shriver Mill and Homestead. He saw almost no difference in its appearance today from when he had seen it with his parents.

Joseph slid back to the main part of the wagon and pulled Ben with him. Joseph whispered to Ben, "I saw you looking at the Shriver Homestead. Did you see the house up on the hill to the left?"

Ben went to take another peek and returned to Joseph. "Yes," he responded. "What about it?"

"Those two houses are owned by brothers. One of the brothers supports the Rebels and the other supports the Union. They each have children fighting in opposing armies. Louis Shriver is a friend of mine. He lives in the big house on the right. I play with him whenever I come to visit my uncle. He is about your age,'' Joseph explained to Ben.

"Do Louis' father and uncle fight with each other a lot?" Ben asked.

"No, not that I have seen. As a matter of fact, the brother who supports the North owns slaves and the brother who supports the South doesn't."

"That doesn't make sense," Ben said.

"I know, but it's true," Joseph stated.

"Are those the same Shrivers that own the general store?" Ben asked.

"They are probably related somehow," Joseph answered. Then he added, "We just passed the road that goes to my uncle's farm." He looked carefully out of the back of the wagon. He wiped the dust from his face before speaking again to Ben, "No miracles today. The other wagons are still there. We're here to stay."

The boys leaned back, frustrated. Neither said a word as the wagon rumbled along. After a few minutes, Joseph tapped Ben. "Listen to that," he instructed Ben.

"What am I listening for?"

"Can't you hear those cannon blasts?" Joseph asked.

Ben listened carefully. It was hard to pick out specific sounds with all the noisy wagons rumbling. But soon Ben felt certain that he could hear the cannons. He said to Joseph, "If we can hear the sound from thirty miles away, imagine how loud the cannon blasts sound in Gettysburg."

Suddenly, a deep, strong singing voice filled the air. It was the driver of their wagon. Ben knew the song the man was singing.

> Yes, we'll rally 'round the flag, boys,
> we'll rally once again.
> Shouting the battle cry of Freedom.
> We will rally from the hillside,
> we'll gather from the plain.
> Shouting the battle cry of Freedom.
>
> The Union forever, hurrah, boys, hurrah!
> Down with the traitor, up with the star;
> While we rally 'round the flag, boys,
> rally once again.
> Shouting the battle cry of Freedom.

Other voices from other wagons joined in with the singing. The boys' driver led the other men in singing song after song for an hour or more. It helped make time go more quickly for Ben. Ben could sense the great emotions the songs made the soldiers feel. Some seemed to give the men courage to face whatever danger lay ahead, while others seemed to make the man miss their homes and loved ones so much that even Ben was on the verge of crying. Joseph sang along in a soft voice. The wagon started to cool off slightly as the sun sank lower into the western sky. The sounds of battle grew louder as the boys came closer to Gettysburg.

Before long, an order was shouted from several wagons in front of the boys' wagon. The order was sent back from driver to driver in domino fashion, bringing all the wagons to a halt. Ben's heart started to race. This might be the moment to escape. But Ben was afraid to move. If the wagons were ready to unload, the boys would be caught for sure. Joseph seemed to be waiting to see what would happen next. Without the sound of the wagons, the battle noise was clear and threatening. Ben was fearful that the driver would hear his rapid breathing in the quiet moments between cannon blasts.

Joseph dared to look outside. He whispered back to Ben, "We're in Littlestown. Maybe the wagons are going to stop here for the night."

Ben nodded in agreement. The boys lay quietly waiting for the soldiers to make a move. If the driver was stopping at an inn to eat, the boys would have a chance to escape. Ben was trying to make up a story he could tell the soldiers if he were caught. He wondered if he could convince them that the wagon driver had kidnapped Joseph and him.

Their driver soon got off his mule. Ben and Joseph crouched, ready to spring out of the wagon. But within seconds, their wagon was surrounded by the voices of several other soldiers. They were complimenting the singing of the boys' driver. Some were complaining to one another about how sore their rear ends were from sitting on their mules for so many hours.

There was no way the boys could escape. It looked as though they would soon be caught. Then word went around from soldier to soldier. New orders had been received telling them to hurry on to Gettysburg. The dinner break they were expecting had been quickly cancelled. There was much groaning as the drivers went back to their wagons.

"Maybe we better make a run for it now," Ben suggested.

"Wait," warned Joseph. "It should be dark soon. The darkness will keep anyone from seeing us run away."

Ben didn't agree. He felt that now was the best time, but before he could do or say anything, the wagon started rolling again. He hoped Joseph was right. Ben felt very hungry. He remembered the bag of candy that was in his shirt. He pulled it out and started eating. Seeing that, Joseph started eating his own candy. Ben tried to make the candy last a long time. He ordered himself not to chew any of the hard candy, only suck. Joseph had no such plan. He gobbled his down as quickly as he could.

The light in the wagon was growing dim. Ben could not see Joseph clearly. He also noticed that the battle sounds were steadily decreasing in frequency. *It must be getting too dark for the soldiers to fight any more today,* Ben thought. He tried to estimate how much longer the ride would be to Gettysburg. He remembered that it took about ten minutes to drive from Littlestown to Gettysburg when traveling at about 45 miles an hour. That would mean that Gettysburg was about eight miles away. Then he tried to figure out how fast the mule was pulling the wagon. He guessed that they might be going about five miles an hour. So the trip would probably be about an hour and a half or more. Soon he could hear no more battle sounds.

Ben said to Joseph, "We'd better catch some sleep while we can. I think we will have to do a lot of running tonight to get away from Gettysburg before the fighting starts again in the morning."

"I feel all slept out from my nap this afternoon," Joseph said.

"At least try to sleep. The first one to wake up should wake the other. All right?"

"All right," Joseph agreed.

Ben found it difficult to sleep at first because of the rocking and bumping of the wagon. He tried packing more straw around and under his body to absorb the shock. That helped enough to let his muscles relax, and he was able to fall asleep.

Sooner than Ben wanted, Joseph nudged him. It seemed to Ben that he had only slept a few minutes, but it had been longer. The wagon was not moving. From nearby, he could hear a man shouting, "Get the lanterns over here so we can unpack these wagons. Quick, hop to it!"

Both boys looked out the back of the wagon. It was very dark, but they were able to see the outlines of the wagons, thanks to the glow of the moonlight.

"It's now or never," Joseph said.

Each boy quickly, but silently, climbed out of the wagon. Ben tried to blend in with the shadows. A horse near them whinnied, but none of the soldiers paid much attention. There were so many drivers around that there was no place to run that would be safe. Ben crawled under the wagon to look for an escape route. Joseph stayed close to him.

Upon surveying the situation, Ben could see that he and Joseph were in the center of the wagon train. More and more wagons were arriving each minute. He tapped Joseph's shoulder and pointed to a tunnel formed from the many wagons parked side by side. Soldiers walked hastily between the wagons, but if the boys timed their rushes well, Ben felt that they could crawl from the underside of one wagon to another without much chance of being seen.

There was a wooded area at the edge of the roadway. They should aim for cover there. Joseph smiled and nodded as Ben told him of his plan.

Finally, Ben saw a gap between the bustling soldiers. He took a deep breath, then ordered Joseph, "Go, now." He grabbed the younger boy's sleeve and pulled him along to the next wagon. They were safe. Ben's heart beat faster and harder.

Joseph was ready for the next rush before Ben was. Ben felt himself being tugged out into the open and shoved under the next wagon closer to the woods. Now there were no more wagons left between the boys and the trees. But a group of soldiers was coming toward their hiding place with lanterns in their hands. The boys didn't have much time. Those lanterns would light up the area well enough to expose their hideout, but there were too many soldiers near the wagon to run. Fear filled Ben's body. Joseph held onto Ben's arm in a frightened vice-like grip.

Suddenly, the men with the lanterns circled a wagon twenty feet away from where Ben and Joseph hid. A soldier ordered, "I need you men to help me unload this wagon over here."

The soldiers that were near the boys ran over to help. When the way was clear, Ben and Joseph scurried into the woods. The shadows of the trees hid them well. Fortunately, Joseph had kept his hold on Ben. If he had gotten separated from Ben, Ben doubted they could have found each other due to the sudden darkness of the forest where no moonlight entered.

Ben said to Joseph, "We need to follow the road back to Westminster, but we must stay out of sight."

Joseph said, "We can just run from one tree to another. I can see the road from here. Can't you?" Ben looked. The white stones of the moonlit highway seemed to glow. It would provide an excellent guiding light.

All of a sudden, a pair of soldiers stepped within a few feet of the boys. There had been no warning. These men had emerged out of the dark thickness of the forest. Ben and Joseph didn't move a muscle. Fortunately, they were not seen. Ben looked into the forest. In the distance, he could see the glow of small campfires. It would be easy to avoid the soldiers entering the woods from the road because they could be seen early enough. However, the soldiers coming out of the darkness would be a problem for the boys.

Joseph and Ben moved carefully. First they listened for the snapping of any nearby twigs. Then they looked carefully before racing to the cover of the next tree along the highway. Whenever a soldier came near, each pressed himself like moss against the nearest tree.

Progress was very slow. Ben estimated that they were traveling less than one mile an hour. Brambles in the undergrowth tore at his legs. Low hanging branches scratched his face. He could hear the "ooch's" and "ouch's" of Joseph suffering the same torment. Eventually, they came to an open stretch of fields. Many campfires were scattered about, looking much like big fireflies signaling to the little fireflies that blinked in the night air above the field. There would be little cover for the boys in this great openness.

Ben got down on his belly and showed Joseph how to crawl along the ground as he had seen soldiers do in old war movies. He inched along on his elbows and knees, trying to keep the road partially in sight so he wouldn't get lost. Joseph followed him. Ben's hands landed on sharp stones, prickly plants, and some moist, gushy things that he didn't want to identify. Suddenly, Ben's right elbow sunk into a soft warm lump.

"Ouch! Hey, what do you think you're doing?" a man's voice shouted at Ben.

Ben froze for a moment as all the soldiers in the area looked to see what had happened. Fortunately, Ben and the complaining soldier were out of view, thanks to the high grass. Ben spoke in his most manly voice, "Sorry. I didn't see you. I'll just sleep over here. Good night. See you in the morning."

"Well, just don't let it happen again," the sleepy soldier ordered.

Ben moved over a few feet and lay down as though he were sleeping. Joseph had already flattened himself out on the ground when he heard the commotion. No one had seen him. The boys lay there for several minutes until Ben felt it was safe to go on. He vowed to himself that he would try to be more careful. Joseph crawled up to where he had heard Ben's voice last and found him ready to go.

At the edge of the field, Ben could see that there was a house set on the side of the road, right in the boys' way. Lanterns hung from the porch rafters. The blue coats of the soldiers resting on the porch chairs were like warning signs to the boys. Ben and Joseph had to wriggle their way around the back of the house, climbing under fence rails, around sleeping hogs, and through a flower garden. Soon the house was behind them. The boys were safe so far.

As they traveled southeast, there were fewer and fewer groups of soldiers. Fatigue was setting in rapidly. Hunger pulled at Ben's stomach. It was fear alone that kept the boys moving. Dew was settling down on the field grass. Ben's and Joseph's clothes became damp and cold. Joseph finally said, "I have to stop and rest. We will be safe here."

Ben wasn't sure about that, but he was exhausted too. He was willing to take a chance. "Maybe we can stop for a little while. But let's try to wake up in about an hour."

"Good," said Joseph. The boy immediately sprawled out on the ground and went right to sleep.

Ben had never slept on the bare cold ground before. He gathered as many leaves as he could to use as a mattress. He curled himself up in as small an area as possible, keeping his hands and feet close to him for fear that some wild animal might come and nibble on his fingers or toes. Fortunately, sleep came quickly.

CHAPTER 7

JULY *2nd*, 1863

Joseph's scream woke Ben up. Before Ben had time to open his eyes, he felt himself grabbed by the pants and pulled up to a standing position. He looked. It was dawn and there stood two, very muscular, tall Union soldiers. One man held Joseph with one hand and Ben with the other. The other soldier pointed a rifle first at one boy, then the other. "You're under arrest. Don't try to run or I'll have to shoot," said the man with the rifle.

Ben felt like crying. How could they have been caught now? Did these men follow them since they left the wagon? What would happen now?

Joseph's eyes squinted in anger. "You can't arrest us. We didn't do anything wrong. You'd better leave us alone or I'll tell my brother on you."

"We can arrest you — and we are arresting you — so be quiet!" ordered the man holding the boys. He continued, "Finkner, here, and I have our orders to stop any deserters and bring them back to Colonel Vincent. You are lucky no one shot you yet. What company are you with?''

"We aren't soldiers," Ben explained. "My name is Ben Leeds and this is Joseph Harner. We live in Westminster and we're just trying to get home.''

"Sure," said the soldier with the gun. "You can tell your story to the colonel.''

The boys' hands were tied behind their backs and they were swiftly marched back down the road towards Gettysburg. All the struggle of walking and crawling the night before had been in vain. It now looked like they might be shot, put in prison, or forced to fight in the battle. As the first ray of morning sunlight hit Ben's eyes, the sound of a gunshot broke through the morning air. Finkner howled and grabbed his earlobe. Drops of blood trickled down onto his shoulder.

"Hit the ground!" he ordered. The boys and the other soldier obeyed. "Darn sharpshooters. They must be hiding in those trees over there. Wouldn't you know they would start so early in the morning." He picked up his rifle and aimed at a tree to the west. He shot twice. A man in tan clothes fell out of the tree, picked himself up and limped rapidly away. "Come on, let's get out of here," Finkner commanded as he held a handkerchief to his ear. He didn't seem to be hurt badly.

There was a great deal of activity along the highway. Soldiers rushed here and there in groups. Cannons were being pulled off the road and onto the bordering fields. They were aimed westward. The only fighting heard so far was an occasional distant shot of rifles. Ben wondered when the heavy fighting would start for the day.

The boys were guided into one of many tents in a small field near a creek. This tent was large and sturdy looking. A man could stand up straight in it. The other tents had looked more like small pup tents. A serious looking man sat at a small wooden desk set in the middle of the room. He was busily talking to two other soldiers who were standing at attention. He stopped when he saw the boys.

Finkner saluted the man. "Colonel Vincent, sir, Private Finkner reporting."

The colonel nodded his head and the private continued, "While on sentry duty, Private Arbaugh and I found these two deserters. They refuse to tell us what unit they are with."

Colonel Vincent looked at each boy. "What do you have to say for yourselves?"

Joseph blurted out, "You are in big trouble now. We aren't soldiers and we didn't do anything wrong."

Ben agreed, "He's telling the truth. We got on one of the supply wagons from Westminster to hitch a ride, and then we couldn't get off until it arrived at Gettysburg. We need to go home as soon as possible. Our parents will worry."

"They are a bit puny looking to be soldiers," said Colonel Vincent as he looked the boys over.

"Don't let their size fool you, sir," said Private Arbaugh. "We have some drummer boys younger than this little one in our own unit." He lay his hand on Joseph's head.

Joseph ducked. "Don't touch me. I'm going to tell my brother."

"He is a tough little guy, isn't he?" the colonel remarked to the other men. They nodded. Then he turned back to face Joseph and Ben. "How old are you boys?"

"I'm nine and a half and Ben is almost twelve," Joseph replied.

"Private, these boys are too young to be soldiers. This little guy and his brother ought to be home with their mother," the captain declared.

"Ben's not my brother. He's my friend," Joseph said. "My brother is Sergeant Andrew Harner of the 6th Michigan Cavalry commanded by Brigadier General George Custer."

"Sir, the 6th Michigan is my unit," said one of the other soldiers who stood in the tent. "I know Sergeant Harner."

"Well, then, find him and have him claim these children," ordered the colonel.

"I can't, sir," the soldier replied.

"Why in blazes can't you?"

"Because my brother is still in Westminster with a broken ankle," Jospeh cut in.

The soldier told the colonel, "That's right, sir. If this child knew that, then he must be who he says he is."

Colonel Vincent looked at Private Finkner. "Why are you bringing me civilian children? Take them out of here now before they get hurt."

"Where should I take them, sir?" asked the sentry.

Ben asked, "Could someone take us back to Westminster, please?"

"We can't afford to let any of our soldiers leave Gettysburg. We are preparing for a big attack by Lee's men today. Take the boys back where you found them, then go back to duty. This time, only pick up prisoners who don't need their mothers to rock them to sleep at night," the captain ordered.

Ben and Joseph glared with anger at the soldiers. Their hands were unbound, and they were led by foot back to the field where they had been captured.

"Here you are, boys. The rest of the trip is up to you," said Private Arbaugh.

"What if some other guards try to arrest us?" Ben asked.

"Here are passes the colonel gave me to give to you. Don't lose them. If you don't have them and some guard should stop you, he may not be so easy on you." He handed each of the boys a folded sheet of paper. Ben stuck his in his pocket after making sure the pocket didn't have a hole in it. Then the boys set off.

The nearby countryside was swarming with busy soldiers. In another field far to the west, Ben and Joseph could see the Rebel army equally busy. Thousands of men in each army were working to prepare for the coming battle. Hundreds were building stone walls that Ben figured would be used to protect the soldiers as they shot at the enemy. Many had no stones to work with, so they were chopping down trees and using the logs to make walls. Dozens of men were pulling cannons into position over the rocky fields. Some

Annelle Woggon Ratcliffe 1/90

men just ran back and forth over the battlefield for no reason that was clear to Ben. He understood now why army ants were given their name. These soldiers looked like ants overrunning a spilled oatmeal cookie. Sniper fire continued on and off, but it was never aimed towards the boys. Ben figured the Rebels were only shooting at blue targets.

The boys headed south. Suddenly, an explosion shook the earth. Ben and Joseph both grabbed their ears in response to the tremendous noise. Then all was silent. Joseph gave a weak smile, "I guess that's what the cannons sound like from close up." The still smoking cannon was only 20 yards away from the boys. The men who had fired the cannon were already seated on the ground, talking to each other in a calm manner. The boys went closer to look.

"Has the battle started?" Joseph asked.

"Not yet, sonny," one of the men replied. "We are just shooting towards them Johnnies every once in a while so that they know we're still here waiting for them. You'd better get out of here. No civilians are allowed on the battle field, especially children."

"Come on, Joseph," said Ben. "We still have time to get to safety."

It was late morning and the boys had a long journey ahead. Ben's feet were tired already. Joseph didn't seem to be as tired as Ben.

"Joseph, I'm going to try hitch-hiking. Maybe one of the wagons will give us a ride." Ben stood by the side of the road and held his thumb out pointing south. No wagon driver paid any attention to him. Ben felt guilty trying to hitch-hike. He knew his mother would say it was very dangerous and that he might get kidnapped. But in a war situation like this, especially in the 1800's, it seemed unlikely that the boys needed to fear being hurt by criminals.

"What are you doing with your hand?" Joseph asked.

"This is how to let someone know that you need a ride."

"Not around here it isn't. You've got to call out to them and tell them what you want," Joseph informed Ben.

So Ben tried shouting to the next wagoner. "Excuse me, sir. We need a ride."

The driver looked at Ben and called to the boys as he passed by, "Can't stop now. We all have our orders to stop at nothing so that we can bring supplies to the troops."

Ben decided to give up. The boys walked for a long time without talking. Each just looked straight ahead and walked as quickly as possible. Without warning, Joseph ran up a nearby hill to a clump of weeds.

"Get back here!" Ben called. "We can't stop now."

"You keep walking if you want to, but I'm going to eat some of these black raspberries. I'm starved," Joseph replied.

Ben hesitated. He had been able to ignore his hunger until Joseph mentioned food. He tried to figure out how far they had walked. He could see that there were very few soldiers in the fields here, though the road continued to be busy with supply wagons. Ben was not as fearful of being captured anymore now that he had a pass. He decided to join Joseph just for a few minutes. The rest and food should give him enough energy to go on at least a little while longer.

The berries were delicious. The boys' arms became lined with scratch marks from the berry bushes' thorns, but it was not easy to be careful picking when their frantic hands found it difficult to fill their mouths quickly enough.

Eventually, they slowed down as their hunger was relieved. Joseph started to stuff his pockets with extra berries. Purple juice began to stain his pants. Ben decided not to say anything since the harm was already done. He felt certain there would be other berries along the roadside, so he didn't try to save any for himself.

The journey continued. The sun beat down on Ben's head. His hair hung in clumped strands, sticking to his sweaty forehead. Soon Ben started limping. He felt like his feet had blisters on their blisters.

Joseph, who was walking ahead of Ben, turned back to see why his friend was slowing down. "I think you would do better walking barefoot," he suggested.

"I thought of that a long time ago," Ben said, "but I don't think my feet can stand all these sharp stones on the road."

"Then walk on the grass along the side of the road."

Ben felt pretty stupid for not thinking of that first. Maybe his brain didn't work as well when it was being fried. He sat down and took off his shoes and socks. He felt instant relief. The grass on the roadside felt cool on his aching feet.

They walked for another hour. There were still no heavy

battle sounds in the distance, only the single cannon burst once from the Union side every ten or fifteen minutes with a responding cannon firing from the Confederate side. Ben was glad that the explosions seemed to be less deafening. That meant he and Joseph must be making good progress in getting away from Gettysburg.

"Look," Joseph said. "There's a stream over there. Let's get some water to drink and swim for awhile." He didn't wait for Ben to respond. He just slipped off his shoes and long pants and ran to the stream. He lay down in the shallow water and let the cool water pass over his body. He opened his mouth and let some of the water rush in.

Ben was extremely thirsty too. He didn't even stop to think about whether it would be all right to stop. He ran to the stream, but did not take off his pants. He was too afraid that someone might see him. He drank until he could see his belly bulging. Then he and Joseph hunted for crayfish. They found some under the bigger rocks and caught them, but the boys released them when they realized they had no way to cook them.

Then the boys decided to build a little dam so they would have a deeper pool of water to swim in.

GA-BLAM!

Ben dropped the rock he was holding. Joseph slipped on a rock and fell into the water.

GA-BLAM!

GA-BLAM, GA-BLAM! The ground continued to shake. Ben looked off to the north. He could see a stream of smoke rise in the air after each cannon blast. Each flying shell made a whistling sound in the air and then made a loud explosion when it hit its mark.

"Sounds like they mean business this time!" Joseph exclaimed as he picked himself up.

The cannon blasts were joined by rifle fire. There was constant noise now. Ben covered his ears. "Let's get out of here!" he shouted to Joseph.

"Wait for me," called Joseph as he grabbed his clothes and came running after Ben.

It was impossible for Ben to tell how far away the battle was. The roar of the explosions echoed off the hills. Smoke filled the air like a huge cloud over the Gettysburg area.

With a last burst of energy, the boys raced towards Littlestown. Neither felt the pain of stones on their feet. They dodged soldiers on horseback and supply wagons. They kept running until they could no longer hear the rifle shots, only the cannons. Then Joseph put on his clothes. He sat down on the side of the road to catch his breath.

"Come on, Joseph. We have to keep moving," Ben pleaded.

"I'm so tired, I don't care if the whole Rebel army comes to get me," Joseph sighed. "And if I don't eat pretty soon, I'll die before the Rebels get me anyway."

Ben looked around for more berries. He didn't see any, but in the distance, he could see a field that appeared to have a crop of something edible. "Just walk as far as that field over there," Ben pleaded. Joseph agreed reluctantly.

It was surprising how slowly the boys walked, even when food was in sight. Each had spent all his energy. It was late afternoon, probably near supper time. When they got to the field, Ben saw rows of bean plants. He had never eaten raw beans before, but he was ready to try. Joseph pulled bean after bean off the plants and stuffed his mouth. Ben ate too. He saw a cornfield nearby, but when he ran over to look, the silk on the ears of corn was still green. It would be weeks before the corn would be ripe.

When Ben got back to Joseph, the boy was sprawled out on the ground, fast asleep.

"You can't sleep now," Ben told Joseph as he started to shake the sleeping boy. But Joseph did not respond. The only way Ben could tell Joseph was alive was by the slow, peaceful rise and fall of the boy's chest.

Ben thought, *What am I going to do now?* He was tired too, but he couldn't stand the thought of sleeping on the hard ground again. His body still ached from the night before. He looked around the surrounding countryside. He listened. The furious sounds of battling cannons continued. He knew that each blast was sending men to their graves. It was too horrible to think about.

Wagons continued to pass by Ben. He figured it wouldn't hurt to try asking for a ride again. He stood up and walked out to the road. He stepped out in front of an approaching wagon. He waved his arms to try to get the driver to stop, but the driver just whipped his horses on and cursed at Ben. Ben was able to jump out of the way just in the nick of time. When the next wagon approached, Ben was more careful. He stood on the side of the road and called out, "Please stop! We need help!"

The wagon stopped. "What's the problem here?" the driver asked in a gruff voice.

"My friend and I need a ride to Westminster. We've been walking for hours and we can't walk any farther. If we stay here, we may get caught in the battle."

"Sorry," the man said, "I've got wounded soldiers in here that need to be taken to Littlestown for treatment. Any wagons you see along here will be carrying more wounded. There is no room for you." He made a clicking sound with his mouth, and the horses took off again. Ben was not able to see into the wagon, but he could hear a chorus of groans over the sound of the wagon rumblings. He was glad he could not see the source of the groans.

Ben looked around again. This time he noticed a red brick farmhouse set back in a small grove of trees at the far end of the field in which he stood. A small drive ran alongside the field, ending at the house. Next to the house was a large barn and a smaller shed.

Ben longed for a soft haystack to sleep in. He tried to wake Joseph again, but Joseph refused to waken. Ben took a deep breath and picked Joseph up in his arms. The younger boy was very heavy. Joseph wriggled a bit, wanting to be left alone, but Ben held on tightly. Slowly, Ben walked toward the barn. He hoped that the farmer who owned the property would not see him. There appeared to be no flicker of light from the farmhouse.

The barn door was open. Once in the barn, Ben found it difficult to see well. His eyes took a few minutes to adjust to the reduced lighting. Finally, he was able to see a ladder that was nailed to one wall. It led to a loft. The smell of hay came from that direction. The odor of manure was also in the air. He heard the mooing of a cow. There were three stalls, each with a cow standing in it. He saw no horses. The floor was made of hard dirt, like his basement floor back in Westminster. Straw was spread about over the dirt, creating cushioning for his sore feet.

Ben's strength left him. He set Joseph down. The sleeping boy curled up on the floor. Ben felt he should try to get Joseph on some clean straw, but he was unable to get Joseph to move. Instead, Ben picked up a handful of clean straw from one side of the barn and stuffed it under Joseph's head for a pillow. Then Ben climbed the ladder and crawled into the loft. A few chickens cackled and flew out of his way. There, in front of him, lay a glorious pile of hay. He thought of Little Boy Blue and was soon fast asleep.

CHAPTER 8

JULY 3*rd*, 1863

"**H**ey, you. Wake up!" said a girl's voice below Ben's loft.

Ben opened his eyes. He knew Joseph was awake too, because he heard Joseph say, "Where am I?"

"You are in my barn, that's where you are. Why are you here?"

"I don't know," Joseph responded.

Ben kept quiet. He wanted to see how things went before he let anyone know he was there.

The girl said, "Goodness sakes! Do you have amnesia?"

"I don't think so. I remember my name," said Joseph.

"Well, what is it?"

111

"Joseph Harner. I live in Westminster, Maryland. Ben and I are walking home."

"Who is Ben?" she asked.

Ben peeked over the edge of the loft. He saw a girl with waist-long, honey-colored hair. Freckles almost covered her face. She seemed to be close to Ben's age. She wore a loose brown dress that went below her knees and she wore a long white apron over it. In one hand she carried a bucket, and in the other she held a basket. Two other buckets were standing beside her.

"Here I am," Ben announced.

Joseph and the girl looked up.

"Are there any more of you?" the girl asked.

"No," both boys responded.

"Well, my name is Jenny Powel. If you help me milk the cows and gather the eggs, I will try to talk my parents into letting you have breakfast with us."

"That sounds good to me," said Joseph.

"I'll gather the eggs," Ben offered. He didn't have the slightest idea how to milk a cow.

"There may not be many eggs today," Jenny informed him. "The hens don't like all the battle noise."

Joseph took the bucket from Jenny. I'll milk a cow if you hold

Annelle Woggon Ratcliffe 1/90

onto her. Where is the milking stool?''

Jenny pointed to a little, three legged stool sitting in the corner of the barn. Then she led a cow out of the stall and tied her to a post in the center of the barn floor. Joseph put the stool down on one side of the cow and started to milk her.

"Were you in the battle yesterday?" Jenny asked.

"No, we got out of there just in time," Joseph said. He told her about their past two days. Ben filled her in on the parts that Joseph had slept through.

Jenny listened attentively, reacting with just the right amount of gasps and "Oh, my's". She said to the boys, "I wonder what will happen if the Rebels win this war. Do you think they will make all of the Northerners prisoners?"

"Naw," said Joseph. "There aren't enough jails in the world to hold that many people."

"Don't worry," said Ben. "The Rebels won't win."

"How do you know?" Jenny asked.

"Just trust me. I know," said Ben.

Jenny looked at Joseph. He nodded his head in agreement with Ben. Jenny shrugged her shoulders and asked no more questions.

The first of the three cows was milked. It took about another half hour to finish milking the other two. Ben was having problems locating the hens' eggs. Each hen had made her own little nest in various areas of the barn. None gave up her eggs easily to Ben. They squawked and tried to peck at his hands. He had gathered about a dozen eggs when he heard a loud boom from a distant cannon. Ben flinched in surprise, squashing the egg he was holding in his hand. He wiped his hand on his trousers.

"Here we go again," said Jenny. "When will the battle ever end?"

"I'm pretty sure it will end today or tomorrow. I can never remember if the Battle of Gettysburg lasted three or four days," Ben said.

Jenny peered at Ben. Then she picked up a bucket of milk and said, "I'll go on ahead of you two to break the news to my parents about your being here. They are really nice. I'm sure there'll be no problem. I'll come back for you." She left.

"What do you think?" Ben asked Joseph.

"I think we are going to get a good free meal in a few minutes. I'm starved."

The cannon blasts continued. Ben and Joseph pet the cows because they looked so scared. Jenny soon returned. "Come on. Bring the eggs and the rest of the milk."

The boys followed her. Jenny's father stood on the back porch of the house. He had hair the color of Jenny's. He also had a flowing red beard. His eyes were gentle, happy eyes and so green that Ben found it hard not to stare at them.

"Welcome," he said. "Mrs. Powel will have breakfast ready in a few minutes. You can wash there at the pump." He pointed to the pump near the shed. "Jenny, you bring the eggs and I'll carry the milk into the house." Another cannon sounded. "I wish they would stop all that noise. My cows are giving me less and less milk each day. I've already had most of my field hay trampled by the soldiers who camped out here a couple of days ago." He took the buckets from Ben and Joseph and went into the house.

Ben asked to pump the water when Joseph and he went to clean up. Ben still got a thrill out of pulling the lever up and down, never quite knowing when to expect the water to start gushing out. The boys washed as the water poured out of the spout. Ben could hear the windows of the house rattling with each distant cannon explosion.

"Do you think the fighting will come in this direction?" Joseph asked Ben. "There sure is a lot more traffic on the pike today than yesterday."

"There should be no danger between here and home," said Ben, even though he was not sure. He didn't want Joseph to worry. "Let's eat."

The boys were met by Mrs. Powel as they entered the back door of the house. She was a heavy set, short woman. Her hair was brown with wisps of gray fringing her face. Her dress was of the same fabric as Jenny's. She probably sewed both dresses herself. She also wore a white apron, but hers was much larger and had red and purple stains splashed over the front. In each hand, she held a platter of food. One platter was stacked high with pancakes, and the other held a small mountain of scrambled eggs. The aroma was wonderful.

Apparently remembering his manners, Joseph said, "How do you do, Mrs. Powel. I am Joseph and this is Ben."

"Nice to meet you young men." Her attention was suddenly drawn to the clattering windows in the room. She looked back at the boys and said, "We will try to hold our house together until the end of breakfast. Come in to the table."

"Thank you," said Ben, showing that he knew how to be polite too.

"Need any more help, Mother?" Jenny asked as she entered the room.

"Just bring in the bowl of raspberries and strawberries. Then I think we will be set to eat."

The five sat around a square wooden table. There was no table cloth like at the Harner's house. A blessing was said over the food and the eating began. There was no table-talk. Everyone concentrated on the eggs, pancakes, milk, and berries.

When stomachs were well satisfied, Mr. Powel spoke. "What are your plans now, boys?"

Joseph answered, "Sir, I guess we will keep on walking. We ought to make it home in two days."

"Son, you can't go on that road today. Didn't you see what was out there this morning?" Jenny's father asked.

"Just more soldiers and wagons," Joseph replied.

"Union guards are bringing the first Rebel prisoners from the battle. It is pitiful. Go look out the front window."

Joseph, Ben, and Jenny excused themselves and hurried to

the front parlor window. There they saw a long line of tired, sad looking men walking south along the highway. Many had blood stained bandages wrapped around different parts of their bodies. Many were barefoot. Some were helping to support the weight of their more crippled friends. The group of prisoners currently in front of the farm had to jump off to the side of the road as several swiftly moving wagons passed them. One wagon had no cover over it, and Ben was able to see wounded men packed closely together, some sitting, but most lying down. Through the open parlor window, Ben could hear the men groaning and crying out in pain at each bump the wagon hit.

"Father," called Jenny. "This is terrible. Isn't there anything we can do to help those poor prisoners?"

Joseph said, "I don't feel sorry for them. They were caught trying to kill our soldiers. If they weren't where they are now, who knows how many more of our men they would kill?"

Jenny looked angrily toward Joseph. "Look at those prisoners. They are hurt and tired and probably hungry. Some, most likely, have children at home like you and me. Now they may never see them again."

Joseph didn't seem to know what to say.

Mr. Powel said, "It is sad, Jenny. But I don't want you children out there. Some of the prisoners may try to escape and there could be some shooting. I don't want you to get hurt."

Ben noticed that the group of prisoners that jumped off the road was still there. One of the two guards watching them started walking up the Powel's driveway.

"Mr. Powel, sir, I think you should come here and take a look at this," said Ben.

Mr. Powel left the table and came to the window. Mrs. Powel followed. Jenny's father saw the guard. "You children go into the kitchen and help Mrs. Powel clean up. I'll take care of this."

"Now you be careful, James Howard Powel," his wife warned.

He smiled at her, "Yes, dear."

Out on the front porch, he stood with his hands crossed over his chest as the guard approached him. Mr. Powel greeted him politely, "What can I do for you today, stranger?"

The soldier paused. He was not used to civilians being nice to him. "I need food and water for me and my partner."

"What about for your prisoners?" Mr. Powel asked.

"They don't deserve any," the soldier responded.

"I have very little food to offer you. Your soldiers took all our extra food on the march to Gettysburg. Our wheat has been trampled by your men. Our animals have all been stolen, except for a few hens and cows. But I will give you all the water you can drink and all the cherries you can eat if you will share them with the prisoners," Mr. Powel offered.

"You know, I don't need your permission. I could just take whatever I want."

"Yes, I know, but I am asking you, as a fellow human being, to share the food with your prisoners. They are humans too." Mr. Powel said.

The soldier didn't reply. He just stood there thinking. Mr. Powel took advantage of that hesitation and grabbed a basket off the front porch. He started pulling cherries off the big tree in the front yard. He shouted toward the house, "Children, come out here and help me."

The kids had been watching everything. Mr. Powel gave them each a bucket and told them to start picking cherries. Mrs. Powel and Mr. Powel filled two other buckets with water and started to ladle drinks to the men. The guard followed Mr. Powel, but didn't make any objection.

"May we please sit down while we eat?" one of the prisoners asked the other guard.

"There's no time!" the guard barked.

Mr. Powel stared at the guard. He said, "A five minute rest will give these men enough energy to travel better for you."

The guard huffed, "All right, just for a few minutes. But don't expect any more rest stops."

The tired men sat in the cool morning grass and hungrily ate the cherries the children brought to them from the cherry trees in the back yard. Suddenly, one of the guards shouted, "Halt, or I'll shoot!"

Ben looked up and saw that one of the prisoners had tried to make a run for the small grove of trees on one side of the Powels' field. The man didn't stop, so the soldier aimed his rifle.

"Get down, children!" Mr. Powel shouted. But Jenny ran to the guard. She pushed the barrel of the rifle up as the shot went off.

The angry guard pushed her away and aimed again. The other guard was busy pointing his rifle at the remaining prisoners to keep them from escaping. The runaway prisoner was out of sight. The guard started to chase after him, but his partner called, "Don't leave me alone with these men. We have enough here to keep us busy."

"He was just our drummer boy," explained one of the prisoners. "He never lifted a gun in his life. He won't be any danger to your soldiers."

"Blast it all," the guard shouted at the remaining prisoners. "If anyone of you tells anyone about this, I'll haunt you forever." Then he looked at Mr. Powel. "If you find that boy and help him, I will personally have you arrested and put into prison with him." To the prisoners he said, "The rest of you, get moving. This farmer, here, says you should have some energy now that you have eaten. Let me see." Off they marched.

"What's going to happen to them?" Jenny asked her father.

"I imagine that they will be marched to a prisoner-of-war camp where they will stay until the war is over," he responded.

"At least they won't have to fight anymore," Ben added.

"Ah, but they will have to fight," Mr. Powel said. "They will have to fight every day to keep their spirits up long enough to survive the stress of prison. For many men, the thought of not seeing their families again, possibly not for years, is more than they can bear."

The sounds of the battle continued. Covered wagons rolled by, followed by more groups of prisoners. Mr. Powel broke the sad mood by saying, "Children, there are chores that need attending to. With the three of you working, we should be able to finish early enough to give you boys a ride to Westminster this afternoon.''

"I will do any chores to keep from having to walk any more," Joseph admitted. Ben agreed.

"Jenny, please go in the garden and pick a half bushel of beans for your mother. Ben and Joseph, you each grab a basket, and we will pick peas, potatoes and cabbage. Maybe we can pick enough to sell in Westminster. Do you think people there would buy fresh vegetables?'' Mr. Powel asked.

"I'll bet they would," Joseph said. "There are hundreds of soldiers there, and the town must be very short of food by now."

Ben added, "The soldiers might take it from us before the civilians can buy it."

"Then I guess we will have to be careful to get it into the right hands, won't we?'' Mr. Powel smiled.

Each person did his or her assigned chores. The sun was rising toward mid-sky. The weather was hot and dry. Mr. Powel loaned each boy a straw hat to keep the sun off his head. Ben and Joseph had filled twenty or more bushels with vegetables when the lunch bell rang. The boys asked Mr. Powel if they could stop work to eat.

Mr. Powel laughed as he saw how eager the boys were to eat. He hemmed and hawed, watching the boys fidget. Then he gave them permission to go. The boys washed up and went into the house.

"What smells so good?'' Joseph exclaimed.

"We made some cherry pies," said Jenny. "Mother thought we could sell a few in Westminster."

The kitchen was very hot from the heat of the stove combined with the summer heat, so the family and the boys ate the noon meal out on the shaded back porch where there was a small breeze. Bees and flies buzzed about, but only Ben seemed to notice. They ate baked chicken, green beans, corn bread, and milk.

"How many chickens do we have left now?" Mr. Powel asked his wife.

"Seven hens and one rooster," she replied.

"Then we'd better not eat anymore of them. We will need the ones we have to start another brood once the soldiers leave the area."

"Then what do you suggest I make for supper?" she asked.

"Maybe I could shoot a few squirrels," he suggested.

"But some of the soldiers on the road might hear you and think you are firing at them. You could get shot," she said.

"You're right about that, dear," said Mr. Powel. "I could go out to the creek and try to catch some fish, but then I wouldn't be able to drive the boys home."

"I could drive them, Father," Jenny offered. "I know the way."

"I don't want you out there alone with all those soldiers," he said.

"But Ben and Joseph will be with me for half of the trip. If we leave soon, I could be home before nightfall."

Mrs. Powel said, "Dear, maybe she could get on the back road to Taneytown and then cut over to Westminster. That way she might avoid the military traffic."

"I can't be certain that there are fewer soldiers on that road," he responded. "No, it is too dangerous to let the children go without an adult."

Ben said, "There wouldn't be much reason for soldiers to be on that road. The reason your road to Westminster is so busy is because the only supply trains for the battle come into Westminster. Taneytown wouldn't be as important to the army right now."

"That sounds logical," Mr. Powel said.

Ben felt Mr. Powel might be giving in a little so he suggested, "Maybe you could ride as far as the road to Taneytown with us. Then you could see if there are any soldiers there. If there aren't, Joseph and I can go ahead with Jenny, and you can walk back to the farm and go fishing. If there are too many soldiers, Joseph and I could stay here until the battle is over, though...," Ben signed, "our mothers will probably be terribly worried."

Mr. Powel wiped the sweat from his brow with the back of his arm. "What do you think, Mother?"

"I think the boy makes sense. You go ahead with the children to make sure they will be safe."

"All right," Mr. Powel agreed. "You children pack up the wagon with the vegetables and pies. Then you can help me pull the wagon along the cow path to the back pasture."

"Why do we need to pull it?" Joseph asked.

"The army probably took all his horses," Ben suggested to Joseph.

Joseph looked very worried. "Then how are we getting home? Is the cow going to pull the wagon?"

The Powels looked at each other and smiled. Jenny said to Joseph, "We keep Brooks, our horse, in the storage shed in the back pasture. We let him out at night to graze so the soldiers won't see him. All our other horses were taken."

"Won't somebody try to take Brooks from us if we take him to Westminster?" Ben asked.

"We will have to take that chance," Mr. Powel said. "You children will have to be very clever."

"Maybe we could rub some dirt into his coat to make him look old and sickly," Joseph suggested.

"Good idea. And be sure to travel slowly, as though Brooks is too weak to go any faster," Mr. Powel added.

Jenny's mother said, "You folks better get going. Jenny, I'll be expecting you home before dark."

"All right, Mother," said Jenny as she hugged and kissed her mother goodbye.

The boys thanked Mrs. Powel for her hospitality. They loaded the small buckboard wagon. Then the children and Mr. Powel pulled the wagon over the bumpy cow path. Progress was slow.

The wagon wheels got stuck several times along the way. The four had to rock the wagon back and forth until it could be drawn out of each rut. When they arrived at the shed, Brooks whinnied with joy at being released during the daytime. He let the children cover his coat with mud and dust without any objection.

Mr. Powel harnessed the horse to the wagon. Then he climbed into the driver's seat and picked up the reins. "Jump into the back of the wagon, boys, but watch out for the food." Jenny sat on the driver's seat with her father. Mr. Powel flicked the reins up and down, called out, "Giddy-up," and away they went.

CHAPTER 9

AFTERNOON
JULY 3rd, 1863

Brooks had to use all his strength to pull the wagon over the lumpy pasture. The horse stretched his head forward, putting his whole body at such an angle that Ben imagined the horse shooting like a rock in a sling shot if the harness should break. Ben and Joseph had to hold on very tightly to the sides of the wagon to avoid being bumped off.

"Will we be going through Littlestown?" Ben shouted to Jenny loud enough so he could be heard over the wagon rumbling.

"No, we are going to avoid it by taking this short cut through the field over to the road to Taneytown. It's about six miles from here to Taneytown," Jenny said.

"How far is it from there to Westminster?" Joseph asked.

"I'm not real sure," she answered.

Ben said, "It's about 10 miles. I saw a road sign once, right outside of Westminster, that had the mileage to Taneytown printed on it."

Then Jenny pointed out something in front of them. "See that line of trees up there at the edge of the field? That's where the road to Taneytown is."

Within a few minutes Mr. Powel drove the wagon onto the road and headed southwest.

"Look, Father. There aren't any soldiers here." It was true. The only traces of life on the road were the deep wheel ruts that had been gouged into the soft mud during the last rain storm, and then had dried as hard as rock, like fossil prints, from the sun's baking heat. The sounds of cannons blasting still echoed through the countryside. Ben figured that must have scared all the farm families into their homes to wait out the battle.

Mr. Powel drove the wagon about a quarter of a mile down the road before he stopped. "Looks like you children can handle this road. But promise me, if you see a large group of soldiers, no matter what color uniforms they are wearing, you will turn around and come straight home."

"Yes, Father," Jenny said. The boys nodded their heads. So Mr. Powel handed the reins to Jenny, kissed her on the forehead, then jumped off the wagon and walked back towards the farm.

Ben called out to him, "Don't worry, Mr. Powel. We'll be O.K." Jenny's father smiled and waved at the children, then turned and walked away.

Ben and Joseph climbed onto the front seat with Jenny. As they

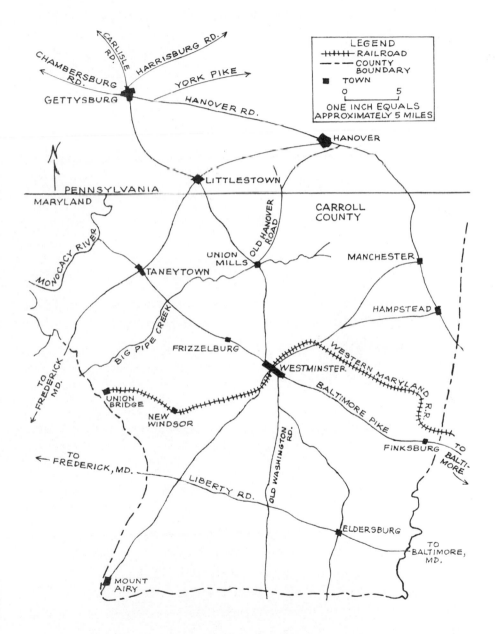

LEGEND
++++ RAILROAD
— — — COUNTY BOUNDARY
■ TOWN
0   5
ONE INCH EQUALS
APPROXIMATELY 5 MILES

rode along, they still saw no soldiers on the road, but the children could see that many soldiers had been this way. Fence posts had been pulled out of the ground, and the fence railings were gone. They had probably been used for firewood, the children decided.

Suddenly, as they passed a patch of berry vines, a teenage boy jumped out into the roadway. He had been hidden from sight until that moment. "Stop!" he shouted.

Brooks reared as Jenny pulled on the reins. "Whoa, boy. Settle down, boy." Then she shouted at the teenager, "What do you think you're doing scaring my horse like that? Get out of here!"

"Oh, please stop. You've got to help me," the boy pleaded.

Ben looked more closely. The boy was wearing a gray Rebel shirt, but he was wearing brown homespun pants like the ones Ben and Joseph wore. He had no cap. Instead, he wore a blue bandanna wrapped around his forehead as a bandage. It was stained with dried blood. His feet were bare.

"Hey," Joseph exclaimed, "you're that runaway prisoner from this morning, aren't you?"

The young soldier recognized the children. He relaxed a little, remembering the kindness of the Powels. "Yes, I am. You helped me this morning. Won't you help me now?"

"What do you want us to do?" Jenny asked.

"I need to get back to Virginia. Please give me a ride in your wagon."

"But your army is just a few miles north of here. Why don't

you go back to them?'' Joseph asked.

The soldier lowered his head and said, ''I refuse to go back to that battle. I will never, ever go back!''

''But we can't take you all the way to Virginia. We are just going to the next town on this road,'' Jenny explained.

''Then take me that far and I'll walk the rest of the way. You can tell me how to get to the Potomac River from there. Once I get across that, I'm safe.''

''But if you are caught by Union troops, you will be arrested again, and if you are caught by your own army, they may shoot you for being a deserter,'' said Ben.

''That's why I need your help.''

''What's your name?'' Jenny asked.

''I'm Sam Parker,'' he responded. The other children introduced themselves.

Jenny said, ''I think we should give him a ride to Taneytown. From there, he could walk to Frederick and then to Harper's Ferry.''

''I know my way home from Harper's Ferry,'' said Sam.

Ben warned, ''It's 50 or 60 miles from Taneytown to Harper's Ferry. You can't walk that far.''

''Sure I can. I walked here from my home in Winchester, Virginia. That was at least 100 miles.'' Sam laughed when he saw

Ben's mouth drop open in surprise.

"Come on," said Jenny, "but first get rid of that shirt. If we are caught helping you, we will be put into prison too."

"Thank you. I promise I will alway be grateful for your help." Sam took off his shirt and stuffed it under a raspberry bush. He climbed in the back of the wagon and off the children went again.

"I heard from the other prisoners this morning that you are a drummer boy," Joseph said to Sam.

"I was a drummer boy," Sam muttered. "I always thought it would be so exciting to have my own drum and play a marching beat for the army. It was fun at first, but then we came here to fight a real battle. You can't imagine what it was like to have to stand out on the battlefield with cannons and rifles firing all around you. I watched hundreds of men get shot. All I had was a stupid drum to beat on to give them courage. I couldn't protect them or myself."

The children listened, picturing themselves in Sam's place.

"There I stood, banging on my drum. Heck, they couldn't even hear me with all the artillery noise. On the first day of battle, we were winning. But yesterday afternoon, nobody seemed to be gaining much ground. Each side was just blowing up the soldiers on the other side."

Jenny wiped a tear off her cheek.

Sam continued, "The captain I was standing near was hit by a bullet. I just dropped my drum and stood like a statue. I didn't know what to do. Then a bullet whizzed past my head, scratching it a bit. That's all it took for me to know that I had to run for my life. I quickly found out how many big rocks there are on that battlefield, because I think I either tripped over or hid behind most of them. One time, I tripped and fell between two huge boulders and got wedged into the space between them.''

''What did you do?'' asked Joseph.

''I stayed there for hours. I just let the battle go on, knowing those rocks would protect me. I kept my eyes closed so that I wouldn't have to know what was happening. But I couldn't keep out the terrible sounds. Finally, the battle moved away from the area. I could hear the cries of wounded men all around me. One of the wounded was right next to me, trying to pull himself into the protection of the rocks where I was. He had been shot in the leg. He was surprised when I moved to help him. He said that he thought I was dead because I had been lying so still. I let him lean on me and I helped him off the field, but some Union men rode up and arrested us. That was it. As soon as the battle ended for the day, they started marching us down toward Jenny's farm. They said they were taking us to Baltimore.''

Jenny said, ''I'm so glad you weren't hurt. It must have been like a nightmare for you.''

''I wish it was only a nightmare,'' said Sam. ''Then my friends would come back to life in the morning.''

''How old are you?'' Ben asked.

''Fourteen.''

The children continued talking. As they got closer to Taneytown, they saw that almost every crop in the surrounding fields was destroyed. It looked like a tornado had ripped through the area. Ben said, "There must have been thousands of soldiers camping out here. They sure didn't leave much behind them."

When they pulled into Taneytown, there was much more activity than there had been outside of town. Small groups of soldiers were busy working at one job or another. There appeared to be no danger since no one paid any attention to the children. Most of the townsfolk went on with their daily business, avoiding contact with the soldiers. Ben could barely hear the artillery fire from Gettysburg anymore.

At the crossroads in the middle of town, Jenny said to Sam, "This is where you get off. We're turning east here. If you go straight, you will eventually get to Frederick. But be sure to ask for directions as you go. There may be a few turns in the road that I don't know about."

Sam shook Ben's hand and Joseph's hand and gave Jenny a gentle hug.

"Here," said Jenny, "take one of these pies with you in case you get hungry." Sam thanked her.

Then Ben had an idea. He took off his boots. "I'll bet these will fit you," he said as he handed them over to Sam. "But watch out. You might get blisters from them."

"Thank you," Sam said. "I don't think I'll get blisters. I think my feet are two huge callouses anyway." He tried on the boots and they fit. Sam got out of the wagon and the children watched him walk away. He turned once to wave goodbye and then continued on his journey home.

"Move along," shouted a voice from a buggy behind the children's wagon. "You're holding up traffic."

"Sorry," Jenny called back to the driver of the buggy. Quickly, she started Brooks off towards Westminster.

As they rode along Jenny asked the boys, "Do you think Sam will get home safely?"

"I think so," Ben answered. "There shouldn't be many soldiers on the route he is taking. Most are in Gettysburg now."

"I hope you're right," said Jenny. "He was just a couple years older than you. How would you feel fighting in a war?"

"I never really thought about that before," Ben answered. "I guess I would hate to have to walk for hundreds of miles, take food from strangers, and face the chance of getting killed in battle. I couldn't stand to watch people get hurt."

Joseph said, "If I were in the army, I would want to be in the cavalry like my brother."

"I didn't know you had a brother in the army," said Jenny. "I used to have a brother."

"What happened to him?" Joseph asked.

"Two years ago, when he was five years old, he cut his arm on a rusty nail that was sticking out of the wall in the barn. He got 'lockjaw'. The doctor called it tetanus. My brother got so sick that he died."

"He died from a little cut on his arm?" Ben asked in disbelief.

"Yes. It wasn't much more than a scratch."

Why didn't he get a shot of medicine to make him better?" asked Ben.

"Our doctor said there was no cure for lockjaw," Jenny replied.

"Where I come from, all children get a shot when they are little to keep them from getting tetanus," Ben said.

"I thought you were from Westminster," Jenny said.

Joseph said, "Ben is new to Westminster. They probably have better doctors where Ben used to live."

"Well, it's too late to help my brother now. Since then, I've been really careful to watch where I am walking, and my father and mother still keep their eyes out for any rusty metal in our yard."

They traveled on. Ben was hot and very thirsty. Knowing there were fresh pies behind him made Ben hungrier than usual. "Jenny, do you think your mom would let us eat one of the pies?"

"I'm sorry, Ben. I really have to try to earn some money for those pies. We will need to buy a lot of new animals to replace the ones stolen by the soldiers. I hope you can wait a little longer. We are almost to Westminster. We can get food there."

Joseph interrupted, "Look at that." He pointed to a Union soldier climbing up a wooden post that had been stuck into the ground. He had a coil of wire hanging over one shoulder. "What do you suppose he's doing?"

"Looks like he is putting up a telephone line," said Ben. "I thought you said you didn't have telephones."

Annelle Woggon Ratcliffe 1/90

Jenny said, "Those are telegraph lines. My father told me they were hanging some in Littlestown too. The wire is strung for miles and miles to send messages. Electrical signals, that have been sent by one person, travel along the wire, and the message is decoded by a man at the other end of the line."

The soldier, who was up on the pole, saw the children watching him. He called to his partner, who was sitting on his horse nearby. The soldier on the horse then rode over to the wagon.

Ben and Jenny tensed up. Joseph calmly watched the man. Jenny said, "I hope we aren't in some kind of trouble. What did we do wrong?" she asked the boys. Each boy shrugged his shoulders. They didn't know.

When the soldier arrived, he directed his attention to Ben, assuming he was the oldest. "What are you doing out on this road. Don't you know this is a war zone?"

"The only fighting we know about is in Gettysburg. Is there fighting here too?" Ben asked.

"No, but important military activity is taking place here. All travel on this road and in Westminster is restricted," the soldier replied.

Joseph said, "Our home is in Westminster. If we don't go home soon, our parents will worry."

"Then get along. But before you go, did you see any suspicious travelers on the road west of here?"

"No," the three children answered together. The soldier waved them on. For the next several miles, the road became increasingly crowded with soldiers on horseback, empty supply wagons standing by the side of the road, and campgrounds for the soldiers stationed in Westminster.

"I don't like the looks of this," said Ben. "Jenny, you'd better turn around and go home now. Remember, your father made us promise. Just let Joseph and me off here."

"Ben, we're almost there. It won't hurt to drive one more mile into town. That's where the customers are for my vegetables and pies."

Ben felt torn. He couldn't decide which would be more important, honoring his promise to Mr. Powel or helping Jenny raise the money that the Powels needed so much. He hesitantly said to Jenny, "I guess it wouldn't hurt to go a little farther."

For awhile, the soldiers ignored the children. The men were all too busy with their own tasks. But right on the town limits, one fat soldier approached their wagon. "Halt!" he ordered. "Do you have a traveling pass?"

"No, sir," Jenny responded. "I didn't know I needed one. I'm just taking these boys home. They live here in Westminster."

"You can't go any farther unless you have a pass."

"Wait a minute," said Joseph. "We have passes." Ben and Joseph showed their passes to the men. Jenny looked surprised. The boys hadn't told her about their passes.

The soldier read each pass carefully. "These passes are only for you two boys. The girl has to leave."

"But..." Joseph started, but the soldier held up his hand to stop Joseph from talking. He rode his horse around the wagon, looking at the food in the baskets that were sitting in the wagon. Then he stopped his horse in front of Brooks. He got off his mount and approached the dirty horse. He rubbed Brooks' flank and looked at the horse's teeth.

"This ain't too bad an animal. I sure could use a new horse," the man said.

Jenny gasped. "You can't have my horse!" she shouted.

"I can, if I want to," the man announced.

"Wait a minute," said Ben, trying to speak calmly. "Jenny needs this horse to get her back home. You say you need another horse, but I'll bet your own horse isn't really so bad, and it might take a long time for you to break in a new horse. I was thinking that your friends back in camp would be mighty grateful if you brought them back some cherry pies. They might even pay you. Would you consider food instead of the horse?"

The soldier looked as if he were trying to make up his mind.

Joseph warned the man, "If you don't agree, I'll tell my brother on you. He is an officer in the Union Army and he is right here in town. If he finds out you were stealing from civilians, especially children, he will have you court-martialed."

"Aw, he couldn't do anything to me," the soldier responded, avoiding eye contact with Joseph. "But I've decided to take the food and let the little missy go with her filthy horse. Mind you, I'm not scared of anyone's brother."

"Good," said Ben. The boys jumped down from the wagon and set the pies on the side of the road. Then they went back to Jenny as the blubbery soldier greedily tried to pick up all the pies at once.

"Quick, Jenny, get going before more soldiers come. Thanks for all your help. Maybe we'll see you again sometime," Ben said. Joseph said "goodbye" to Jenny too. Then she turned the wagon around and headed toward Taneytown again.

The boys walked into Westminster along Main Street. They were stopped three more times by guards, but their passes worked in letting them through. The activity around the train station was no different than when the boys were last there. The only difference was that many of the wagons coming into town had wounded soldiers in them.

"I wonder where they are taking the wounded?" said Joseph. "We don't have a hospital in town."

"They will probably take them by train into Baltimore," Ben said.

Ben and Joseph finally arrived at Joseph's house. Joseph tried to open the front door, but it was locked. He knocked, but no one answered.

"Stop all that racket out there!" Mr. Flint called from his front window. "Can't you see no one is home. I wouldn't be surprised if your mother left you, you rotten little boy."

Joseph ignored the man. He ran around to the back yard. The yard was being used as a campground for a small group of soldiers.

Looking up and down the row of houses on the block, Ben could see that most yards were occupied in the same manner, all except Mr. Flint's yard. Butch was still standing guard and growled as soon as he saw the boys. The back door of Joseph's house was open, so he and Ben walked in. Joseph called out, "We're home. Where is everybody?"

"Not so loud," Andrew called back from the parlor. Ben and Joseph went in to see him. He was still on the sofa where they had last seen him.

"Why didn't someone open the front door for me?" asked Joseph. "Where is Mother?"

"I still can't get up because of my ankle. Mother is at the Union Meeting House helping with some of the wounded soldiers. The community has turned it into a temporary hospital."

"When will she be home?" Joseph asked.

"She should be here soon. She promised she would take time to come home and make supper for me. By the way, how was Uncle Abe?"

"We never saw him," Joseph answered. Then he told his brother the whole story, with Ben adding a piece here and there.

"That sounds like quite an adventure," Andrew said. "Mother will be glad she didn't know all that was happening."

"How is your ankle today?" Ben asked Andrew.

"The swelling has gone down, but it still hurts a lot whenever I move it."

"Ben and I can make supper for you and Mother," said Joseph. Andrew decided to let him, knowing that Joseph was a very good cook for his age.

Ben went out in the yard to get firewood. The wood pile was gone. The soldiers had apparently used it all. He returned to the house to tell Andrew and Joseph.

"There is some wood in the basement that I was using to build something, but we could use it for the fire. I'll get it," said Joseph. He brought an armload of wood back up to the kitchen. He said to Ben, "I saw a crock of sauerkraut on the shelf in the basement. Would you bring it upstairs to have with our supper?" Ben did.

While Ben got the crock, Joseph started a good fire in the stove. Then he went into the pantry to find more food for supper. There was nothing left on the shelves except a big bag of cornmeal.

"Where's all the food?" Joseph called to Andrew.

"In the stomachs of those soldiers you see outside. Mother and I have been eating cornmeal mush and canned fruit.

Joseph was mad. "I'm going outside to give those men a piece of my mind! How dare they take our food!"

"Wait!" warned Ben. "Maybe they can help us. I can see that they are experts at finding food. Is there anything you need to turn that cornmeal into something that tastes good?"

Joseph thought, then said to Ben, "If I had a couple of eggs and some milk, I could make cornbread."

"Then go outside and offer to make the soldiers cornbread if they will give you eggs and milk," Ben suggested.

"That might work. I'll try," Joseph responded. He went out to talk to the men. When he returned, he had all the necessary ingredients, plus a small block of bacon. "Easy as pie!" he announced.

Ben set the table while Joseph cooked. Just as Joseph was pulling the cast iron pan of cornbread out of the oven, Ben heard Mrs. Harner unlock the front door and walk in.

"Land sakes alive, I didn't expect to see you back here," she said to Joseph and Ben. She hugged them both. "The soldiers have the whole town under guard. How did you get back home?"

"I'll tell you soon. First come and have some supper," said Joseph proudly.

"Supper? Bless your little heart," she said. Joseph blushed.

Ben said, "How does cornbread, sauerkraut, and bacon sound?"

"I'm not even going to ask where you found all that food. Maybe it was the same way I got this." Mrs. Harner unwrapped a small package she had been carrying. In it was a cherry pie.

"Where did you get that?" asked Andrew.

A nice soldier brought it over to the meeting house and gave it to the doctor for taking care of his friend. When the fellow left, the doctor gave it to me to thank me for my help."

Ben and Joseph laughed. "We've seen that pie before," said Ben. Ben wondered how many hands that pie had passed through before it got to Mrs. Harner.

While they ate supper, the boys retold their adventure. When they finished eating, Joseph took a pan of cornbread out to the soldiers. When he returned, Joseph asked his mother, "Do you have to go back to the meeting house tonight?"

"Yes. I need to help just one more night. Tomorrow, nurses will be sent out by wagon to care for the wounded. Many of the men will then be transferred by ambulance wagon to real hospitals in Baltimore and Washington. I understand that there are hundreds of severely wounded men being cared for in the homes of the people of Littlestown. It is all so tragic. The stories the men tell me are too horrible to tell you children."

Andrew said, "Mother, why don't you rest for an hour or so before you go back. You have had a hard day."

"Ben and I will clean up the kitchen," Joseph offered.

"I think I might just do that," said Mrs. Harner. "Ben, do your parents know you are home yet?"

Ben had forgotten that he would need another excuse for staying with the Harners. He could think of none. "No, mam. I'll tell them as soon as I can."

"Be sure to go home right after you've finished helping Joseph. When you see your parents, would you please ask them if you may help out tomorrow morning at the meeting house? I will have Joseph there doing errands for the nurses. We could use your help too."

"Yes, mam," Ben agreed.

"Go to bed soon, Joseph. Tomorrow will be a busy day," said Mrs. Harner. "Good night. See you in the morning." Joseph's mother went up to her room.

While cleaning up the kitchen, Ben whispered to Joseph, "I can't stay here tonight. If I go up to your room, your brother will see me."

Joseph answered, "I wish we could sleep in the back yard again, but there's no room now. Let me think."

Andrew heard the whispering sounds. "What are you two up to?" he demanded.

"Nothing," Joseph answered. But the whispering continued. Joseph told Ben, "I've got it. We'll both go out in the back yard and wash up. Then you can come in wrapped up in a sheet from the clothesline. You can carry a rope from the tool shed under the sheet. Andrew won't know it's you, especially if you stoop over until you are my height. When you get to my room, you can let one end of the rope down to me and I'll climb up."

"Don't you think the soldiers will be suspicious?" asked Ben.

"They will probably just think we are playing."

Their plan worked. Andrew was busy reading a book when Ben walked past him. Without lifting his eyes from his book, Andrew said, "Good night, little brother." Ben mumbled a response and quickly proceeded upstairs. At first, Ben had trouble holding the rope while Joseph tried to climb into the bedroom. The younger boy was heavier than Ben thought he would be. So, Ben tied his end of the rope onto the leg of the bed and then sat on the bed for extra weight as Joseph climbed up.

Each boy crawled into a bed. Joseph fell right to sleep, but Ben stayed awake for a few minutes, thinking. He thought about how soft the feather pillow was and how smooth and cool the clean sheets felt on his skin. He never again wanted to be as uncomfortable as he had been the past two nights. He longed to stay in bed for the whole day. He tried to remember what it was like being bored. Would he ever have time to enjoy boredom again? Tomorrow would be another hard day.

CHAPTER 10

JULY *4th*, 1863

The boys did not wake up as early as they were supposed to. The sun was already shining brightly into the window when Ben started shaking Joseph. "Wake up. Your mother said we should go to the meeting house this morning to help out."

Joseph pulled the sheet over his head and tried to go back to sleep, but Ben pulled it back off. Joseph groaned and got out of bed. Ben reminded him again about the work they had to do at the meeting house. This time Joseph listened.

"That's right. We'd better hurry!" Joseph exclaimed.

Ben headed toward the bedroom door. Joseph stopped him. "You can't go that way. Remember, you aren't even supposed to be here. You'd better go out the window. I'll get some of the leftovers from last night's supper and bring them for us to eat."

Ben climbed through the window, and then Joseph pulled the

rope back into the house. Ben turned to see if the soldiers were watching him, but they were all gone. The tent and the horses that had been tied in the alley were also gone. Many soldiers rode back and forth along the alley way, their horses loaded with gear.

As he waited for Joseph, Ben sat on the chopping block and watched the soldiers in the alley. The neighborhood dogs were all barking, but none as loudly as Butch. The German shepherd strained at his leash, trying to bite any soldier that dared to come near his property.

Mary O'Neil stood at the back fence of her yard. She seemed to be barking at the soldiers too. "Where are you going?...Why are you going?...I'll bet the Rebels beat your boys at Gettysburg, and now you're running away. You won't get far. They'll catch you for sure."

Most of the soldiers ignored her. They had more important things to do than to talk to her, but one finally couldn't stand her badgering and said, "Miss, we're just trying to leave this area so we don't have to listen to you."

"I'm going to tell my daddy on you!" Mary wailed.

"Go ahead," he responded. "While you're at it, tell him that the Yankees whupped the Rebels up there in Gettysburg. Maybe you should be the ones to run away."

Mary cried, "Liar!" and she ran back into her house and slammed the door.

Joseph brought Ben a thin slice of cornbread and a cup of milk. Ben told Joseph about the soldiers and Mary, and about the battle being over. Joseph was jubilant. "We won, we won! You were right all along. Let's go tell my mother. She will be glad that the battle is over."

They ate quickly, then set off toward the meeting house a few blocks away. As they walked, Ben started thinking about going home again. He said to Joseph, "I can't wait much longer for that stupid dog, Butch, to disappear so I can go home. We'll have to make a better plan soon."

"My brother has a gun. Do you want him to shoot the dog?" Joseph asked.

"No. It's not the dog's fault that he has a mean master who makes his pet hate people. Maybe there is another answer, like a sleeping potion, or a trap, or something like that."

"First thing tomorrow morning, we can go over to the apothecary and see if the chemist has something you could use," Joseph suggested.

"What is an apothecary?" Ben asked.

"That's a place where you buy medicine."

"I sure hope it has what we need. It's not that I want to leave you, but I don't belong in this century. If I make the wrong move, I might change history, and that could be dangerous."

"Here we are at the meeting house," said Joseph as the boys turned onto a walk leading to a two story, red brick church. A little graveyard sat to one side. Several large elm trees shaded the building from the hot summer sun. Sprawled over the trampled lawn, dozens of soldiers lay on old worn army blankets. Some of the men appeared to be sleeping, but others propped themselves up on an elbow and talked to nearby buddies. Most wore bandages on some part of their bodies.

Mrs. Harner was not in the church yard, so the boys went into the building. When Ben's eyes grew used to the dim light, he could see that wounded soldiers filled up most of the floor space. Two women walked from patient to patient, speaking softly to each and dabbing handkerchiefs to feverish foreheads. Joseph's mother was standing beside the doctor, and the two were in serious conversation. This was not the right time to interrupt.

As they waited, Ben felt a tug on his trouser leg. He looked down. A young, sick-looking man whispered, "Please, bring me water." Ben wasn't sure if he should. His mother had told him it could be dangerous to give some sick people water to drink.

"I'll see what I can do," Ben responded. Ben approached Mrs. Harner.

She turned away from the doctor and saw the boys. "I'm glad you boys are here." Ben told her about the thirsty soldier. She told Ben, "We have a room full of thirsty men. Clean cups are over there in the corner and the pump is out back. You may give water to any man who is able to ask for it. If one cannot speak, then get a nurse to help him."

"Can you go home and rest now, Mother?" Joseph asked.

"Yes," she said. "The nurses have just arrived from Baltimore." She pointed to three women wearing long white aprons over their work dresses. "Let me introduce you to one of the nurses."

Mother walked the boys over to a brown-haired, motherly-looking nurse. "Nurse Wasmer, this is my son, Joseph, and his friend, Ben. They will be helping you this morning. I've already given them the job of bringing water to the men."

Annelle Woggon Ratcliffe 1/90

Nurse Wasmer smiled at the boys. "It will be nice to have two strong young men here to help me. You boys go ahead with your job. I will let you know what other jobs need to be done after that." Mrs. Harner left and Nurse Wasmer returned to her work.

The boys spent all morning filling water cups, running errands for the nurses, and helping to make the patients comfortable. At lunch time, the boys noticed a cook setting up a big iron pot over a fire in the meeting house yard. The cook soon had water boiling and started cutting carrots, celery, onions, and pieces of beef into it. When the soup was ready, the boys and the nurses served a bowl-full to each soldier. Many men had to be spoon fed because they were too weak to eat without help. It seemed to take hours to reach everybody. Joseph and Ben became very hungry while smelling the good soup without being able to eat any.

Eventually the church yard became quiet as men drifted off to sleep. Nurse Wasmer invited the boys to join the nurses for lunch. Ben and Joseph gratefully accepted. Ben felt he had never enjoyed food as much as he had in the past few days, probably because he had never had to go for such long periods of time without food before. He looked down at his belly and noticed that the little bulge that had always been there was flat now.

"We need you boys to wash the dishes while we write up our notes on each patient," said Nurse Wasmer.

This was almost too much for Ben. Of all the jobs he hated, washing dishes was the worst. He leaned over to Joseph, "When do we leave this place?"

"I hope it will be soon. Let's finish the dishes so they won't get mad at us. But first, I'll tell the nurse that we have to leave right after that because Mother needs our help with Andrew."

"Good," said Ben. Joseph talked to the nurse, and then Ben washed dishes while Joseph dried. There seemed to be hundreds of them. One nurse kept bringing them more and more as she scouted the meeting house grounds.

"Where is she finding all these dishes?" Ben asked. "I'll bet she is going door to door throughout Westminster telling people she has two big suckers washing dishes and asking them if they want to donate more."

Joseph groaned in agreement. "I'll never complain about our own dishes at home again — at least not for awhile." The only sounds in the yard were from the clattering of the dishes. Suddenly Joseph stopped drying the dishes. He put his hand on Ben's arm. "Shush...Listen..."

Ben stopped to listen. "What am I listening for?" he whispered.

"Hear that? Someone is crying," Joseph said.

Ben looked around. Under the smallest tree in the yard was a young soldier, probably 15 or 16 years old. He had his face turned away from the other soldiers, trying to keep them from seeing him cry, but Ben and Joseph could see.

"Let's make sure he's all right," said Ben.

"We'd better finish this stack of dishes first," Joseph advised. The boys worked at double speed. The dish nurse did not return with any more. They were done. Free at last.

Ben led the way to the crying soldier. "Excuse me," said Ben. "Are you all right?"

"Leave me alone," the soldier sniffled. He hid his bandaged face in the crook of his arm. "You wouldn't understand."

"How do you know?" asked Joseph. "We're pretty smart."

The soldier looked at them. "What do you know? You're just little kids whose mothers take care of you. All you have to do is run around and have fun. What do you know of war and watching your friends get blown apart? What do you know about getting your face all scarred up so no girl would ever want to marry you? What do you know about being lonely and not seeing your family in almost a year?"

"Well," said Ben cautiously, "we don't know much about those things, but we do know that you are unhappy, and we would like to help you if we can."

The soldier didn't answer.

"Suit yourself," said Joseph. "Come on, Ben. Let's go."

"Wait," the soldier said, as the boys started walking away. "Come back, please. Come sit and talk to me for awhile. I need to forget about what is happening in my life right now."

"Would you like me to tell you a story?" Ben asked.

"Sure, as long as it has nothing to do with war," the soldier replied.

"Ben, tell him a story about the future," said Joseph. Joseph told the soldier, "Ben has some stories about the twentieth century that seem like they could almost happen. It's so real, it seems as though he actually lived in the future."

"Do you mean like Merlin the magician, who lived backwards in time and told King Arthur about the future?" asked the soldier.

"Almost," said Ben. He thought for a few moments and then started speaking in a slow dramatic voice. "I am a time traveler. I have been to Ancient Egypt, Land of the Pharaohs. I have ridden in a chariot by the side of Julius Caesar. It was I who sharpened William Shakespeare's quill pen. I am here today to join you during an important moment in American history; however, my own time — that to which I was born — is the late twentieth century. It is a world that you could never have imagined."

"What is it like?" the soldier asked.

"First tell me, stranger, what is your name? Where do you come from?" asked Ben.

"I am Christian Gunther. I'm from Boston, Massachusetts."

"How long would it take you to ride to Boston from here if you took the fastest transportation you know?"

Christian responded, "I would travel by horse, so I guess it would take about a week."

"Well, Christian, imagine this. In my world, you could travel through the sky, higher than the birds, and it would only take you about one hour to get home from here."

"What an imagination," laughed Joseph.

But the soldier told Joseph to be quiet. He wanted to believe Ben. "Tell me more," he said to Ben.

Ben continued. "Tonight I want you to look up at the moon. Then I want you to picture, in your mind, men from Earth walking around on it. It will be possible for your great-great-great-grandchildren."

"Really?" asked Joseph.

"Do you question me?" asked Ben, very dramatically. Joseph and Christian shook their heads. Ben stopped to take a sip of water and wipe the sweat from his brow. "Ah, it is so hot today. If I were in my own home, I could flip a switch on the wall and a machine would blow cold air into my room and cool me right off."

"Wow!" Christian exclaimed.

"See all those dishes over there that Joseph and I had to slave over to get clean?" Christian nodded. "At home, I would have stuck them all in a machine that would have washed them for me."

"I hope I live long enough to see that," Christian said.

A shadow fell over the churchyard. The three boys looked up. Clouds were gathering in the sky. This helped to cool the air off instantly.

"Ben," said Joseph, "let's try an experiment. Make a list of some things you think will happen in the next few years. Then Christian and I can see if they come true."

"I have paper and a pencil in my backpack," offered Christian. He retrieved it for Ben to use.

"I'll try," said Ben. His knowledge of history was poor, but a few ideas did come to mind. The first thing he wrote on the paper was —

The North will win the Civil War.

"Even I could have predicted that," said Joseph.

Ben thought again. He thought of Abraham Lincoln. But his next thought gave him goose bumps. How could he tell the boys about John Wilkes Booth? They might try to stop the assassination of the president. But then, that would be changing history, and who knows what that would mean to his own family. Maybe he, Ben Leeds, would never have been born. The frustration of having the ability to help Lincoln, but not daring to, tore at Ben's mind.

"Come on, Ben. Write something else down on the list," urged Christian.

Ben continued since there was nothing else to do. "I think I will list a few names of people that will be famous in your lifetime. He wrote:

1. John Wilkes Boothe
2. General George Custer
3. Thomas Edison
4. Alexander Graham Bell

Ben folded the list and handed it to Joseph. "Here," he said. "Put that in your pocket. Check it again in ten to twenty years and see if I was right." Ben didn't want to play the game anymore.

Christian looked at the list first. "I've heard of George Custer already."

Joseph and Ben looked at each other. Joseph said, "Ben told me that we are going to hear a lot more about him in a few years."

"You will just have to wait and see," said Ben.

Christian handed the paper to Joseph to read, then Joseph stuck it into his own back pocket. A few drops of rain fell onto Ben's arms. At that same moment, Nurse Wasmer called to the boys and everyone else who was well enough to help move the wounded soldiers into the meeting house. The rain clouds were building up rapidly and were getting darker and darker.

Some of the wounded were able to hobble into the building without help, but Ben and Joseph were kept busy assisting others into the shelter. The rain became a heavy downpour. The last few soldiers they helped were as wet as Ben and Joseph. The inside of the meeting house was crowded. Benches were placed around the room for any of the wounded who were well enough to sit up.

To Ben, the room felt like a steam bath due to the summer heat and evaporation of water from wet clothes warmed by feverish bodies. The windows could only be left open a crack so the rain wouldn't enter the building. Nurse Wasmer approached the boys again. But before she could say anything, Joseph quickly blurted out, "We really have to get home now. My mother needs us."

She hesitated. Ben guessed that she had wanted them to do more work. "I'm sorry to see you go. You were good helpers. If you see any other children on your way home that might be willing to help, please tell them to come and see me."

"Yes, mam," the boys responded. They rushed out into the rain just as a bright light flashed and a crash of thunder roared through the sky.

Ben grabbed his chest in surprise, looking as though he had just been shot. With a shaky voice Ben said to Joseph, "Let's see if we can get back to your house before the next lightning strikes."

They wasted no time. The boys ran through so many mud puddles that they looked as though they had been mud wrestling. Within three lightning bolts and two thunder claps, they had reached Joseph's back door. The third thunder clap sounded as they entered the house.

Mrs. Harner was busy working in the kitchen. "Well, look what the cat dragged in," she laughed. "Don't go a step farther. Take those wet clothes off and set them on the back porch. Then run upstairs and get some dry clothes on, but don't be too noisy. Andrew is sleeping. I've already had a nap and now I'm getting supper ready. Ben, you stay here until the rain stops."

"Thank you, mam," he replied.

Ben and Joseph got into dry clothes. Then they came back downstairs to help Joseph's mother. But Mrs. Harner wasn't in the kitchen. She stood by the parlor window, looking out onto Main Street. Her face looked sad. She told the boys to come and look too. "It is so sad — so sad," she said.

Ben and Joseph moved the curtain to the side and looked. There they saw the street filled with a parade of exhausted, soaking wet Confederate prisoners. Many could barely walk. The strongest helped the weakest.

"We saw some of them near Littlestown," Joseph told his mother.

"Where do you suppose they are taking them?" asked Ben.

"I don't know. They won't be able to take them much farther

in their condition," Joseph said.

Mrs. Harner said, "They are being taken to the county fair grounds. Yesterday, I saw a group of prisoners being held there behind wire fences. They will stay there until they can be moved to Baltimore, or wherever the military prison is."

Ben's heart felt heavy as he watched. All his thoughts on war in the past had been about heroes, winners, and being on the right side of a battle. Now he could see the losers' side and he felt very sorry for them.

As the boys and Mrs. Harner were watching, there was a sudden commotion. It was difficult to see what was happening because of the darkened sky and pouring rain. There was a flash of lightning that lit up the street enough for Ben to see that the prisoners had stopped walking. A few guards were pointing their rifles at the prisoners while one aimed his rifle at the Harner's house.

"Halt!" he shouted.

"Holy mackerel!" shouted Ben. "Duck!"

The rifle made an explosive sound like a firecracker. No bullet entered the house as far as Ben could see. There was no broken glass.

"Everybody all right?" asked Joseph's mother frantically.

But before anyone could answer, another shot rang out. It sounded as though it came from the side of the house.

"What's happening?" asked Andrew, but there was no time to explain.

The guard shouted again, "Halt or I'll blast ya!"

Joseph got up and ran toward the back of the house.

"Get back here at once!" his mother ordered.

"I want to see what's happening," Joseph called back to her.

Andrew called, "Ben, catch him. Don't let him go outside."

Following orders, Ben chased after Joseph, but the younger boy was already on the back porch by the time Ben caught up to him. Quickly, Ben grabbed his arm.

Joseph shook off Ben's hand and pointed, "Look! They're in Mr. Flint's yard."

Ben looked. There stood the guard, the prisoner, and Butch. Butch was growling and barking ferociously. Mr. Flint heard the noise and came out onto his porch.

"Get this dog away from here or I'll shoot him!" the guard shouted at Mr. Flint.

Mr. Flint was very indignant. He grumbled in his beard as he walked heavily down the wet stairs into the soggy yard. He slipped and fell on his rump, right into a mud puddle, which made him even more angry. Ben and Joseph chuckled to themselves. Mr. Flint got up and grabbed Butch's chain and dragged the dog back toward the house. He held Butch's collar and said, "There, you big, tough soldiers can get by now."

The guard wasn't going to take such rudeness. "Mister, take that dog inside your house. Lock the door and don't show your face again for a least ten minutes or I'll have you arrested.

Mr. Flint grudgingly did as he was told. Ben could see him mouthing rude words to the guard when he was sure the guard wasn't looking. As soon as Mr. Flint and Butch were inside the house, the guard led the runaway prisoner back to Main Street.

"Ben," whispered Joseph. "Look!" He pointed to Mr. Flint's yard.

"Look at what? I don't see anything," Ben said.

"That's the point," said Joseph. "Now is your chance to get back home. Hurry, before Mr. Flint lets Butch out again."

Ben hadn't expected such a quick departure. He didn't know exactly what to do or say. He wanted to say "goodbye" to the Harners even though that meant using up precious time, so Ben ran past Joseph and into Joseph's house to give the surprised Mrs. Harner a quick hug and thanks.

"What's happening out there?" she asked.

"Everything is all right now," Ben assured her. Then he said a speedy farewell to Andrew and ran back outside to Joseph. He looked at his friend. He suddenly knew that he would miss Joseph very much.

"Hurry up," urged Joseph.

"Thank you for helping me. You've been a good friend," said Ben. Then Ben vaulted the fence and ran to the broken basement window. Rain dripped off his nose. He looked back at Joseph and waved before he crawled into his own house.

Ben tumbled down onto the stack of boxes he had placed under the window. When he stood up, he noticed that he was completely dry. He was wearing his own t-shirt and blue jeans again. They felt so comfortable. He heard a knock at the basement door. For a moment he thought it might be Mr. Flint. He prepared for a quick escape, but the door opened and he heard his father's voice, "Supper's ready. It won't stay warm forever. Let's eat."

"Dad," Ben cried, "it's really you!"

"Of course it's me. Come on. I'm hungry."

As Ben started up the basement steps, he heard a voice. "Hey, Ben. I'm coming too." It was Joseph. He was stooping, looking into Ben's house. Suddenly, a loud barking filled the back yard. Joseph screeched and ran away from the window toward his house.

Just then Ben's father shouted, "Your mother is home. I want you up here by the time I count to three. One...two..."

Ben rushed up the stairs. He knew when his father meant business. As soon as he saw his mother, he ran to her and gave her a big hug. Then he hugged this father.

"What was that for?" asked Mrs. Leeds. "You act as though you haven't seen me in weeks."

"If you only knew," said Ben. "You're not going to believe what happened!"

"You can tell us after supper, son. First, we'll sit down and eat. Mother says she has something to tell us too."

During supper Mrs. Leeds told about her day at the hospital. She said, "I had the strangest patient today. He was brought in by an ambulance because he was having a heart attack. Fortunately, he was brought to us in time and he didn't die."

"What is strange about that?" asked Father.

"When I was giving him some medicine, he saw my name badge. He gasped and I thought he was having another attack, but he wasn't. He asked me if I was really Mrs. Leeds. I told him I was. Then he asked me if I had a son or grandson named Ben... Can you imagine that?"

"Have you ever met the man before?" Mr. Leeds asked his wife.

"No. I think I would remember a 88 year old man like that. Ben, have you met any old men while we have lived here?" asked Ben's mother.

"I don't think so. What's his name?"

"Benjamin Harner."

Ben's eyes almost popped out. "Did he have anything else to say?" Ben asked.

"He sure did. He said that his grandfather had told him very strange stories about meeting a time traveler during the Civil War. He said that no one ever believed his grandfather except him. His grandfather told him that in the late 1900's, a boy named Ben Leeds would move to Westminster. My patient told me that he has checked the phone book every year for the past 20 years and has never found any Leeds family in it."

"This sounds very strange to me," said Mr. Leeds. "How could he have found out about our Ben?"

"I'm not sure. He said that he wished his whole family could have seen this day so they would have believed his grandfather, Joseph Harner, before he died."

"Joseph? Dead? It can't be!" Ben exclaimed. "He's in his house right now, next door, hiding from Butch." Ben started choking on a piece of meat. He coughed it out and then sneezed. He jumped out of his seat, excused himself, ran to his room and shut the door.

Ben sat on his bed to think. The shirt he had thrown at the wastebasket earlier was still wadded up next to it. The Nerf ball lay in the corner of the room. Ben wasn't sure what to think. He wondered if he had imagined everything that happened. But he couldn't have. Mother's patient was proof that it really had happened. But would he ever see Joseph again?

Ben started to cry. He reached into his pocket to find a handkerchief, but alongside the handkerchief, he found the piece of old paper he had put in his pocket before going out the basement window. He carefully opened the paper and looked at it under his bright reading lamp. This is what he read.

> *The North will win the Civil War.*
> *1. John Wilkes Boothe*
> *2. General George Custer*
> *3. Thomas Edison*
> *4. Alexander Graham Bell*

Across the bottom of the piece of paper was written:

> *YOU WERE RIGHT.*
> *LOVE, JOSEPH*